THE GREAT EXPLOSION

THE GREAT EXPLOSION

ERIC FRANK RUSSELL

Carroll & Graf Publishers, Inc.
New York

Dedicated to all those who believe that
there is a happy land far, far away.

Published by arrangement with the author and the author's
agent, Scott Meredith Literary Agency, Inc.

First Carroll & Graf edition 1993

Carroll & Graf Publishers, Inc.
260 Fifth Avenue
New York, NY 10001

ISBN 0-88184-991-X

Manufactured in the United States of America

PROLOGUE

When an explosion takes place lots of bits and pieces fly all over the scenery. The greater the wallop the larger the lumps and the farther they travel. These are fundamental facts known to every schoolchild old enough to have some sneaky suspicions about the birds and the bees. They were not known or perhaps they were not fully realized by Johannes Pretorius van der Camp Blieder despite the fact that he was fated to create the biggest bang in human history.

Johannes Etc. Blieder was a lunatic of the same order as Unk (who first made fire), Wunk (who designed the wheel), Galileo, Leonardo da Vinci, the Wright Brothers and many others who have outraged orthodoxy by achieving the impossible. He was a shrimp of a man with a partly bald head, a ragged goatee beard and weak, watery eyes hugely magnified by pebble-lensed spectacles. He shuffled around on splayed feet with the gait of a pregnant duck, who had been making glutinous sniffs since birth and never knew where to put his hand on a handkerchief.

Of academic qualifications he had none whatever. A spaceship bound for the Moon or Venus could thunder overhead as such ships had done for a thousand years and he would peer at it myopically without the vaguest notion of what pushed it along. What's more, he wasn't the least bit interested in finding out. Four hours per day, four days per week, he sat at an office desk. The rest of his time was devoted wholly and with appalling single-mindedness to the task of levitating a penny. Wealth or power or shapely women had no appeal to him. Except when hunting a handkerchief his entire life was dedicated to what he deemed the ultimate triumph, namely, that of being able to exhibit a coin floating in mid-air.

A psychologist might explain this obsession in terms of an experience that Blieder had suffered while resting in his mother's womb. An alienist might define it as the pathological desire of a sniffy-nosed little man to rise high in the world and look big. If he had been capable of self-analysis—which he was not—Blieder may have confessed the thwarted ambition to become an accomplished vaudeville artist. Though he knew nothing and cared less about the wonders of science he did nurse a mighty admiration for professional magicians and illusionists. To him, the greatest glory would be to hold the stage and dumbfound an audience with a series of clever stunts that were not faked, but real.

The actual truth, perhaps, was that bountiful Providence had chosen him to get somewhere in much the same way that other creative imbeciles have been chosen. Therefore he was animated by a form of precognition, a subconscious knowledge that success was sure if he kept after it long enough. So for fifty years he strove to levitate a penny by methods mental, mechanical or just plain loopy.

Upon his seventy-second birthday he succeeded. The coin positioned itself three-eighths of an inch above a pure cobalt disc that represented the output stage of a piece of apparatus bearing no relation to anything that made sense. He did not rush outdoors, yell the news all over town, get blind drunk and paw a few elderly virgins. Instead he blinked incredulously at the penny, sniffed a couple of times, sought in vain for a handkerchief. Then he stacked a dozen more pennies on top of the floater. It made no difference. The column remained poised with a three-eighths gap between the bottom coin and the cobalt disc.

Removing the coins, he substituted a heavy paperweight. The gap did not decrease by a hairbreadth. So he took away the weight and the penny, wondered whether a different metal would produce a different effect, tried it with his gold watch. That also sat three-eighths of an inch above the disc. He fiddled around with his apparatus, making minor alterations here and there in the hope of widening the gap. At one stage the watch vibrated but did not rise or fall. He concentrated on that point, adjusting and readjusting, until he was rewarded with a sound like a sharp spit. The watch vanished, leaving a small hole in the ceiling and a matching hole in the roof.

For the next fourteen months Johannes Pretorius van der Camp Blieder struggled to master his brain-child. Knowing nothing of scientific methods his efforts were determined by guess and by God. In the end he had made every portable item in the house, metallic or non-metallic, float at an altitude of three-eighths of an inch or take off heavenward so fast that it could not be seen to go.

The time had come, he decided, to seek the aid of another and more agile brain. Characteristically, it did not occur to him to appeal to the department of physics of the nearest university. Instead he wrote to The Magnificent Mendelsohn, a top-flight illusionist. This was fortunate; a scientist would have dismissed him as just another crazy inventor whereas Mr. Mendelsohn, as a professional deceiver, was only too willing to take a look at any new swindle in the hope that he could improve upon it and confiscate it for his very own.

In due time Mr. Mendelsohn arrived wearing a theatrical black cloak and a cynical smile. He spent three exasperating days trying to determine exactly how the trick was done. Blieder was no help; he hung around snuffling continually and protesting that he had worked a miracle without being able to explain it. Using his prestige, which was world-wide, Mendelsohn called in two scientists to get to the bottom of the matter and, if possible, turn the apparatus into something more exploitable upon the vaudeville stage.

The scientists came with open minds, looked and saw, tested and retested, checked and rechecked, summoned six other specialists. A slight atmosphere of hysteria developed in the Blieder home as yet more experts were brought in. Finally Blieder himself, frightened and exhausted by the general hullabaloo, handed over his apparatus in return for a guarantee of five percent of whatever profit could be made out of it plus a solemn promise—on which he was most insistent—that the new principle he'd discovered would bear his name forevermore.

Ten months later Blieder died without giving himself time to receive a rake-off. Eleven years afterward the first ship went up powered with what was dutifully called the Blieder-drive. It made hay of astronomical distances and astronautical principles, put an end once and for all to the theory that nothing could exceed the velocity of light.

The entire galaxy shrank several times faster than Earth had shrunk when the airplane was invented. Solar systems once hopelessly out of reach now came within easy grasping distance. An immense concourse of worlds presented themselves for the mere taking and fired the imaginations of swarming humanity. Overcrowded Terra found itself offered the cosmos on a platter and was swift to seize the opportunity.

A veritable spray of Blieder-driven ships shot outward as every family, cult, group or clique that imagined it could do better someplace else took to the star-trails. The restless, the ambitious, the malcontents, the martyrs, the eccentrics, the antisocial, the fidgety and the just plain curious, away they fled by the dozens, hundreds, thousands, tens of thousands.

In less than a century fifty percent of the human race left aged and autocratic Terra and blew itself all over the starfield, settling wherever they could give free vent to their ideas and establish their prejudices. This was the end-product of the obsession of a penny-levitator. It was written down in history as The Great Explosion.

It weakened Terra for four hundred years. Then came the time to pick up the bits and pieces . . .

1

In the days when spaceships had been squirted along by vaporized boron sludge or by cesium-ion jets their size had been restricted by the limits of power available. The relation of payload to exhaust velocity was something no designer dared ignore. Blieder put an end to all that.

Ships rapidly gained a tremendous boost in size and carrying capacity. Planners and builders made it a point of honor that each new vessel must be larger than any of its predecessors. The result was the construction of a succession of monsters graduated nearer and nearer to the popular idea of the super-colossal.

The ship now taking a load aboard for its maiden flight from Terra was the very latest and therefore the largest. Its enormous shell of chrome-titanium alloy was eight hundred feet in diameter, one and a half miles in length. Mass like that takes up room and makes a dent. The great under-belly rested in a rut twelve feet deep.

News-channel commentators, lost for suitable superlatives, had repeatedly described the vessel as "one to make the senses boggle." Always willing to do some fervent boggling, the public had turned up in its thousands. A solid mass of people stood behind the barriers and studied the ship with the bovine stares of good, obedient, uncomplaining taxpayers. It did not occur to any of them that somebody had paid for this gigantic vision or that they had been stung good and hard in their individual and collective wallets.

People were momentarily incapable of deep thoughts about cost. The flag had been raised, the bands were playing and this was a patriotic occasion. It is conventional that one does not think vulgar thoughts of money on a patriotic occasion; the individual who chooses such a time to count his cash is by definition a traitor or a no-good bum.

So the ship lay there while the tribal totem fluttered in the breeze and the bands produced tribal noises and a careful selection of tribal braves filed aboard. Those mounting the gangways numbered more than two thousands. They were divisible into three distinct types. The tall, lean, crinkly-eyed ones were the crew. The crop-haired, heavy-jowled ones were the troops. The expressionless, balding and myopic ones were the bureaucrats.

The first of these types bore themselves with the professional casualness of people to whom a journey is just another trip in a lifetime of meanderings. Lugging loads of kit up the gangways, the troops showed the tough resignation of those who have delivered themselves into the hands of loud-mouthed idiots one of whom stood at the base of the steps and bellowed abuse at every fifth man. The bureacrats wore the pained expressions of those suffering something that shouldn't be done to a dog. They had been dragged from their desks and that is the Last Straw.

An hour after the last man, box, case and package had been loaded the V.I.P. arrived. This was the Imperial Ambassador, a florid-faced character with small eyes and a huge belly. Mounting the rostrum he gazed importantly at the audience, bestowed a condescending nod upon the video cameras, cleared his throat and gave forth.

"With this wonderful ship, the forerunner of many more to come, we are about to establish authority over our faraway kith and kin in their interest as well as in ours. While the opportunity exists and before it is too late we are going to create a cosmic empire of enormous strength and vast magnitude." Cheers. "There is no knowing what formidable antagonists our own lifeform may be called upon to meet at any time in the future and before that happens Earth must reclaim its own so that we can present a common front to the foe. The galaxy contains a multitude of hidden secrets some of which may prove perilous in the extreme when revealed. Together we shall face them and defeat them as Terrans always have done." Cheer. "United we stand, divided we fall. Now is the time to bring our distant parts into unity with the mother world."

He continued in this strain for half an hour, yakitty-yak, yakitty-yak, punctuated by applause. Typically he overdid it to the point of trying to convince himself of the righteousness of his cause. He was full of sherry and in a garrulous mood. The members of the audience grew restless, their cheers became strangled by boredom. They had come solely to witness the ship's departure and this gabby fat man was delaying the ship's departure and this gabby fat man was delaying the event.

Eventually he finished with a gracious word of praise for

God, waved to the audience, bowed to the cameras, tramped up the last open gangway and entered the ship. The airlock closed. A minute later a siren sounded. Without a sound or any visible output of power the ship went up, slowly at first, then faster, faster. It vanished through the clouds.

On board Tenth Engineer Harrison said to Sixth Engineer Fuller, "You heard that speech. What if these kinfolk among the stars don't *want* to be loved by the mother world?"

"Any reason why they shouldn't?" Fuller countered.

"Not that I can think of right now."

"Then why dig up imaginary worries? Haven't you got enough of your own?"

"Yes, I've got one," Harrison admitted. He was a small monkeyish man with protruding ears. "My bike—I'd better tend to it."

"Your *what?*" exclaimed Fuller, gaping at him.

"My bike," said Harrison, evenly. "I brought it with me. I always bring my bike with me."

The first planet showed up like a pink ball on the visiscreens but the effect was a fluorescent distortion; as seen with the naked eye its real color was gray-green. Fourth of a family of nine planets, it circled a Sol-type sun and the whole system lay in a sort of cosmic gap with no near neighbors.

In the chartroom Captain Grayder said to the Ambassador, "According to ancient records this world is the only inhabitable one in the bunch. About a million people were dumped upon it before communication ceased."

"They'll get an awful shock when they find that Terra has caught up with them again," opined the Ambassador. "Which crowd of crackpots picked this place?"

"This," informed Grayder, "is the only world not chosen by its original settlers."

"Not chosen? What d'you mean?"

"They were sent here whether they liked it or not. They were criminals. If any fellow's room was preferred to his company Terra got rid of him by deporting him to where he could share his way of life with his own kind. Let dog eat dog, they said."

"Now that you come to mention it I recall reading something about it when at college," said the Ambassador. "I remember that the history books treated it as an interesting experiment that should solve once and for all the question of whether criminal traits are hereditary or environmental."

"That is why I've been ordered to come here first. Some of

our theorists want to know the answer." Grayder looked thoughtful. "Maybe Terra has another army of no-good bums ready for shipment."

"If so, it's taken long enough to collect them. Four hundred years."

"After a complete clean-up," Grayder pointed out, "it might require several generations for the criminal strain to re-appear."

"If it is hereditary," agreed the Ambassador. "But if it is environmental the clean-up should have had little or no ef-fect."

"I'm no expert myself but I think it's neither," Grayder offered.

"That so? What's your idea about it?"

"When you're born you take pot luck. You are born physi-cally perfect or physically imperfect and in the latter case you're a weakling or a cripple. You're born mentally perfect or mentally deformed and in the latter case you're an idiot or a criminal. I suspect that the majority of criminals could be cured once and for all by brain-surgery if only we knew the proper technique. But we don't."

"You may be right," the Ambassador conceded.

"The great question is that of whether mental deformity gets passed down," Grayder went on. "Whether the sins of the fathers are visited upon the children even unto the third or fourth generation."

"They'll be somewhere around their twentieth generation by now."

"I was merely quoting," said Grayder. He eyed the screen which the glowing ball now half-filled. "We'll know soon."

The Ambassador was silent and vaguely uneasy.

"From our viewpoint," Grayder continued, "the Great Ex-plosion rid our world of a horde of nonconformist nuisances. But, as you can now appreciate, things look mighty different from a ship plunging into space. The home world is far away, lost in the mist of stars. On any new world a Terran is a Terran even though long out of touch and a raving lunatic. He's of the same shape and form as ourselves and that's what counts. He's not of some other and completely outlandish shape."

"All the same, he must be considerably different from us," ruled the Ambassador judicially, "else he wouldn't be squat-ting in the middle of the starfield. A misfit remains a misfit no matter what his shape." He patted his big belly in un-conscious parody of his words. "While I have no resentment against those who deserted the world of their birth neither am I prejudiced in their favor. Let us take them as we find them and judge them solely on their merits—if any."

"Yes, Your Excellency," said Grayder, disinclined to argue. There were, he thought, going to be quite a lot of opinions about what does or does not constitute merit.

Close inspection of the surface provided a surprise as the ship raced around the planet with two thousand pairs of eyes gazing from its ports. Everyone had expected clearly visible signs of human spread and development. Instead, the planet showed evidence of being very sparsely settled.

There were no cities, towns or villages. They caught an occasional glimpse of a ramshackle mass of buildings resembling an old and dilapidated monastery. Almost invariably these were sited upon a hilltop or within the neck of land where a river formed a loop.

No arterial roads could be seen and they were bulleting at too great an altitude to identify footpaths. Several times they swept over great areas of forest and prairie devoid of any sign of habitation. Once they crossed a huge gray desert broken by circular formations of rocky outcrop inside one of which appeared to be an encampment of twenty tents.

The Ambassador sniffed in disgust. "Hardly worth claiming. By the looks of it they couldn't raise six regiments of space-troops much less an effective army. Either they've been decimated by disease or they've found a way to go someplace else."

"I can make a guess why they're fewer than expected," ventured Grayder after some thought.

"Why?"

"History says we shipped a million criminals. I don't recall ever reading how many of them were female."

"Neither do I."

"Seems to me highly likely that women didn't number ten percent of the whole," Grayder added. "Probably the men were in a majority of at least nine to one."

"Not for long," guessed the Ambassador, using his imagination. "In a situation like that a bunch of thugs would slaughter each other wholesale."

"You may be right." Grayder shrugged indifferently. "Let dog eat dog." He peered through the fore observation-port. "We can't go round and round until we're dizzy. Neither can we land just anywhere. A vessel this size needs a long, flat surface and solid bedrock."

"Choose your own place," advised the Ambassador, "but try

to pick it within easy reach of an inhabitation, if possible. We've got to make contact somewhere."

Grayder nodded. "I'll do my best." He picked up the intercom phone and held it in one hand while he continued to watch through the port. After quite a time he said, "This is as good as anywhere," and started barking orders into the phone.

Majestically the monster vessel swung into a long, shallow curve to starboard, losing velocity as it went. Two thousand men bowed, leaned or rolled the opposite way. In the trooper's quarters kit fell out of starboard bunks and dived to port to the accompaniment of general invective. Sergeant Major Bidworthy roared for silence and followed it up with a string of threats. Nobody took any notice.

Completing its curve, the ship drifted to a stop, hung momentarily in mid-air, then began to sink. Its enormous tonnage went down gently and under perfect control in a way that the log-dead Blieder would have considered miraculous. Indeed, even those thoroughly accustomed to such ships never quite got over their sense of wonder at floating down to land, never completely rid themselves of the uneasy feeling that for once something might go wrong and result in one hell of a crash. No Blieder-drive ship had done a dead fall to date— but there always has to be a first time.

So the crew went down with grossly exaggerated *sangfroid* while the troops and bureaucrats descended with queasy stomachs. At fifty feet from the ground Grayder boosted the ship a little forward to position it exactly as he wanted. This caught all but the crew napping. Bureaucrats slid on their official backsides across metal floors, troopers rolled rearward over each other in a mad tangle of bodies, arms and equipment and amid a torrent of oaths. Clinging to a bulkhead, Bidworthy recited the names of those to be shot at dawn. Apparently he was contemplating a massacre.

The ship touched, settled, sank twelve feet deep into hard soil. Crunching, cracking sounds came through the keel as buried boulders split and powdered under great pressure. Power cut off. The bureaucrats picked themselves up with injured dignity, dusted themselves and polished their glasses. The troops sorted themselves out and started surlily restacking their kit while Bidworthy raved at them.

A bell rang in the power-room, the signal to open the port midway airlock. Chief Engineer McKechnie switched on the motor operating the release-gear while Tenth Engineer Harrison went to check that the lock was working properly. He was joined there by Sergeant Gleed, a leather-faced trooper eager to set eyes upon solid earth.

The airlock's outer plug wound inward, swung aside to reveal a pastoral scene that Gleed drank in like a thirsty camel. Lush grassland led from the ship to a broad, sharply curving river on the opposite side of which a large building—or a tightly packed conglomeration of small ones—stood on the neck of land. Something that looked remarkably like a sailing ship's mainmast complete with crow's-nest arose high from the middle of this assembly. In the center of the river one man in a canoe was paddling fast toward the other side.

The lock's phone shrilled, Gleed answered it and Grayder's voice asked, "Who's that?"

"Sergeant Gleed, sir."

"Good! Get down to the river-bank as quickly as you can, Sergeant. There's a fellow in mid-stream making for the other side. See if you can persuade him to come back. We'd like to have a talk with him."

"Shall I take my gun, sir?"

There was a short silence at the other end before Grayder answered, "I don't think you need bother. It would create a bad impression. And in any case you will be well covered by the ship's armament."

"Very well, sir." Gleed hung up the phone, pulled a face, said to Harrison, "Drop the ladder. I'm going out."

"And who gave you permission to do so?" asked a cold voice.

Gleed turned, found himself facing Colonel Shelton, who had just entered the airlock. He stiffened, heels together, hands held rigidly at his sides.

"Captain Grayder told me to go after that fellow in the canoe, sir," explained Gleed.

"Is that so?" said Shelton as though he had every reason to doubt it.

"Yes, sir," assured Gleed.

"Troops are my responsibility," informed Shelton acidly. "I command them. Captain Grayder commands this vessel."

"Yes, sir."

"You are subject to my orders and nobody else's. A man of your rank should be well aware of this fact without the necessity of me telling him."

"I thought—"

"You are not required to think. That task may safely be left to your superiors." Taking the phone off the wall, Shelton added in sinister manner, "We shall see whether Captain

Grayder confirms your claim." Apparently he expected Grayder not to do so, having taken it for granted that Gleed's sole purpose was to sneak out and stake an early claim to wine, women and song. For this estimate of motives Gleed had only himself to blame, being usually the first out and last back on all shore-leaves. But somewhat to Shelton's surprise Grayder did confirm the story. Replacing the phone, Shelton said, "Very well. Get down to the river as fast as you can—you've wasted enough time already."

Resenting that but not showing it, Gleed started to clamber down the ladder.

Shelton said, "Where's your gun?"

"It's here," chimed in Harrison, picking it off the floor and showing it.

"What are *you* doing with it?"

"Holding it," said Harrison.

"That is perfectly obvious," said Shelton sarcastically. "Are you mentally backward by any chance?"

"I suggest you ask Captain Grayder's opinion on that," Harrison retorted. "He is *my* commanding officer."

At that point Gleed scrambled back into the lock, snatched the gun, crammed it into his holster and went down the ladder at top speed. He seemed vastly relieved to be out of it.

Shelton watched him go, then eyed Harrison forbiddingly. "I suppose that not being subject to military discipline you can do pretty much as you please?"

Harrison said nothing.

With a loud sniff Shelton marched back into the ship. He had hardly gone when Sergeant Major Bidworthy clattered into the lock, expanded his chest, took a long, satisfying breath of fresh air. Then he screwed up his eyes for a view of the alien landscape. His face purpled.

"Who said Sergeant Gleed could leave the ship?"

"Colonel Shelton."

"Did Gleed tell you that?"

"No—I was here when he was given the order."

"I'll check on that," warned Bidworthy. "Heaven help you if you're lying to support a liar."

With that, he hustled away in search of Shelton. Behind, Tenth Engineer Harrison shrugged, gazed out of the lock and wiggled his large ears.

Gleed reached the bank just as his quarry hauled the canoe ashore on the other side. The river was wide, slow-flowing and deep. Given enough volume a voice could carry across it. He cupped hands around his mouth and let go with a bellow.

"Ahoy, there!"

The fellow shaded his eyes as he stared across at him. Distance was a little too far for Gleed to make out his features; he appeared to be short, squat and sloppily clothed.

"Ahoy, there!" repeated Gleed, making enticing gestures.

After a moment of uncertainty, the other bawled back, "What do you want?" His Terran words were ancient but understandable. They came to Gleed's ears like, "What dost thou want?" or "What waneth thou?" This did not surprise the hearer who was well aware that four hundred years is a long, long time.

"Come over here," shouted Gleed, trying to make his barrack-square voice sound soft and lovable.

"What for?"

"A talk."

"I am not a gnoit," responded the other mysteriously. So saying, he took something out of the canoe, shouldered it and started up the farther bank. "Wait!"

Focusing for a better look, Gleed decided that the other's burden was definitely a weapon. By hokey, yes, a crossbow. He had seen a couple of them in Terran museums but here was the real article in actual use. Since he had all the modern soldier's hearty contempt for primitive arms it did not occur to him whether he was within effective range of the crossbow. Not that it mattered. The owner was trudging steadily away without showing any inclination to take potshots at him.

"Aren't you coming?" shrieked Gleed, conscious that a number of official eyes were watching proceedings from the ship.

"Wait!" yelled the other again.

Muttering to himself, Gleed found a thick, cushiony clump of grass, sat down and waited. The far-off figure plodded onward, crossbow on shoulder, reached the building or buildings and vanished from sight. Boredly, Gleed studied the place, noticed for the first time that somebody was in the crow's-nest atop the mast. Evidently the erection was a look-out post. He found himself wondering why they considered it necessary to keep permanent watch on a world occupied only by their own kind.

Some time passed before a new figure came into view, walked cautiously to the river-bank and stopped alongside the canoe.

"What do you want?" it shouted.

"A talk—that's all," Gleed gave back.

"Just a talk?"

"Yes."

"What about?"

Controlling his patience, Gleed bawled, "We're from Terra as you can see by our ship. Our captain wants a word with somebody."

"Then let him come over here."

"He wants one of you to visit the ship," insisted Gleed, somewhat exasperated.

"He would. Does he think we're a bunch of gnoits?"

"Look," screamed Gleed, "we don't even know what a gnoit is."

The other digested this information, came to a reluctant decision, said, "We send one man there if you send one man here."

"Why?"

"You kill our man and we'll kill yours."

"Are you nuts?" shouted Gleed incredulously.

"Aha!" riposted the other with the air of having had his darkest suspicions confirmed. "And you have just pretended that you don't know what gnoits are. A liar from the first."

"Why should we kill your man?" yelled Gleed, unwilling to discuss the obscure relationship between nuts and gnoits.

"Why shouldn't you?"

"Because we've nothing to gain by it."

"So you say."

It was now Gleed's turn to bawl, "Wait!" Then he returned to the ship, mounted the ladder, entered the airlock.

"What did you get?" Harrison asked with great interest. "Free beer?"

"Shut up," snarled Gleed. He grabbed the wall-phone, replaced it hurriedly as a thought struck him. "Who should I talk to, Shelton or Grayder?"

"Give forth to whoever answers."

"Yes, that's right," said Gleed, thankful for this easy solution. He reached for the phone again. It rang violently just as his fingers closed around it. The unexpectedness of it made him jump. He rammed it against an ear and said, "Sergeant Gleed here."

"I know," came Grayder's voice. "I watched your return. What has happened? Are they going to send someone here or not?"

"They say we can have one of their men in exchange for one of ours."

"In exchange? Do they think we've come all the way here for the purpose of bartering individuals?"

"They seem to be afraid of us, sir. They say that if we kill their man they will kill ours."

"Holy smoke!" exclaimed Grayder."The idea of slaying a visitor would never cross our minds."

"It appears to be well embedded in theirs, sir."

"Must be something mighty peculiar going on in this world," opined Grayder. "Hold on awhile."

Gleed held on. He could hear a steady mumble of words in the control-cabin as half a dozen people discussed the matter. He recognized the tones of Grayder, Shelton and the Ambassador but couldn't make out a word they were saying. A vague uneasiness crept over him as the mumbling continued. Slowly he incubated the notion that he was soon to cross water. His crystal ball was serving him well.

Grayder came on. "We find nothing wrong with this proposition for an exchange. Obviously any funny business can be made to cut both ways."

"Yes, sir," said Gleed, not liking the word 'cut.'

"So you're it," finished Grayder.

"What was that, sir?"

"You're it. You go over there while their man comes here."

"May I have that order from Colonel Shelton, sir?"

"Certainly."

Shelton came on and confirmed the instructions. "Keep your eyes and ears wide open, Sergeant, and see what useful information you can pick up while among them."

"Right, sir."

"From the males," added Shelton pointedly.

"Eh?" said Gleed, astonished.

"Don't waste your time on the females."

"I hadn't the slightest intention of doing so, sir," assured Gleed in injured tones.

"I believe you," said Shelton. "Thousands wouldn't."

Dumping the phone, Gleed gave it an ugly look. "Officials!" he said.

"No spitting in the airlock," warned Harrison. "Are you staying in or going out?"

"I'm going out. As a hostage."

"A what?"

"A hostage. A full-blown sergeant as swap for a crummy, flea-bitten civilian."

"Well, we've got plenty of civilians aboard," mused Harrison, thinking of the bureaucrats. "One of them would never be missed. Tell Shelton to send one in lieu of you."

"Don't be silly," advised Gleed. "An order is an order and that's that."

He went down the ladder. Harrison leaned out the lock and watched him.

By the time he reached the river-bank a dozen of the opposition had clustered together on the other side. The whole lot had crossbows slung over one shoulder and were gazing expectantly his way.

He cupped hands and bellowed, "I will go over there."

Two of them unhitched their weapons, handed them to their fellows, shoved out the canoe and paddled across. Gleed carefully looked them over as they neared, was not wildly enthusiastic about what he could see. They had lean, peaky faces, beady eyes, tousled hair and were wearing clothes that seemed to have been roughly hacked out of old sacks. It could be said in their favor that they shaved, at least once a month. A real pair of hoboes, thought Gleed.

Coming alongside, they held the canoe to the bank. "Get in."

"Not," said Gleed, knowing his rights, "before your man has got out."

The two grinned nastily at each other. One stepped out and stood on the bank idly watching while Gleed stepped in. Then he followed just as his companion pushed the canoe away from the verge. Both started to paddle like mad.

But Gleed had been a space-trooper too long to be bilked this easily. The canoe had gained only three yards from the bank when he threw his full weight to one side and overturned it. At this point the water was slightly less than four feet deep. Gleed snatched the nearest hobo by the scruff of the neck and dragged him with him as he waded ashore.

The other one was now swimming strongly for the opposite side while the canoe drifted bottom-up downstream. On the farther bank the onlookers howled, shook fists and performed an ungainly war-dance. Three of them unslung their crossbows and started winding them up to full stretch.

Now the captive made a dexterous twist that slipped him out of the ragged jacket Gleed was gripping. He tried to dash for the river but Gleed stuck out a swift foot and tripped him. Saying things under his breath, Gleed grabbed him by the hair, jerked him upright and kicked him in the seat.

This produced more zip in the war-dance on the other side. The yells rose louder. Taking no notice, Gleed got an arm-lock on his prisoner and began marching him toward the ship. Things went *snuck-snuck* past the two of them and the captive promptly tried to throw himself flat. Gleed held him up.

"They're shooting at us," protested the other.

"Then tell 'em to stop," said Gleed.

"Stop!" he screamed belatedly as another *snuck* went past. "Stop you verminous ponks!"

"I couldn't have expressed it better," approved Gleed.

A difference of opinion now arose on the opposite bank, three marksmen boasting of their ability to penetrate Gleed's chitlings without coming near to his companion while the others begged leave to doubt it. The argument became sufficiently heated for one to snatch another's crossbow and smite him over the head with it. The victim had a friend who expressed his resentment forcibly and also got bopped.

Glancing back from time to time, Gleed said, "No discipline in your mob. A real bunch of gnoits, eh?"

The prisoner kicked him in the ankle. Gleed responded with a harder one to the tail and hurried him up. They reached the ladder.

"You first, Mortimer," invited Gleed.

Mortimer jibbed. Gleed seized his hair and bounced his face half a dozen times on the sixth rung. It improved Mortimer's mind if not his features for he proceeded to climb. Gleed mounted behind him.

An escort of four troopers arrived at the airlock just as Gleed and his captive got into it. Taking possession of the latter, they marched him toward the control-cabin. Gleed stood staring sourly at his uniform which was sodden from the waist down.

Harrison observed virtuously, "If I wanted to play in the river I'd get undressed first."

"Your wit prostrates me," rasped Gleed. He stamped around making squelching sounds with his boots. "This isn't all, either. Bet you I'm on a charge for mauling a peaceful citizen."

"I wouldn't be surprised," said Harrison, "seeing that this is your day."

2

In the cabin Grayder, Shelton, Major Hame and the Ambassador surveyed the newcomer with mixed feelings. They didn't like his ratty eyes, his scruffy appearance or anything about him.

"What's you name?" Grayder began.

"Alaman Tung."

Somewhat to their surprise he did not come out with an angry tirade about his treatment. Neither did he refuse to answer questions. He merely stood before them wearing a fixed scowl as though thoroughly accustomed to the idea that in these circumstances protests would be useless. It seemed to the audience that he considered himself a prisoner of war with an unknown fate before him. Obviously he was convinced that Terrans must be enemies and for that he had some basis in the shape of Gleed's boot.

"Where do you come from?" Grayder went on.

"The Tung stronghold."

"Is that the place across the river?"

"Yes."

"You call it a stronghold. By that do you mean it is an official military center, a fort?"

"Fort?" echoed Alaman Tung, screwing up his eyes.

"It is a place to be defended?"

"Of course."

"Against whom?"

"Everyone."

"Everyone," repeated Grayder to the others. "What goes on here?" Without waiting for anyone to guess he said to Tung, "Whoever comes near your stronghold is regarded as a foe?"

"Unless he plays the trading signal."

"Ah, so it isn't *everyone* as you've just said?"

"Everyone all the time except in the trading season."

"How long does that last?" Grayder inquired.

"A few days."

"How often?"

"Once a year. Just four or five days a year. In the spring."

"And what do you trade then?"

"Women," said Tung with devasting casualness.

Grayder was horrified. "You mean you barter females like so much merchandise?"

"Only those who refuse to mate."

His features grim, Grayder said, "What happens to them after they've been traded?"

"It depends."

"That's not an answer." Grayder smacked a hand heavily on his desk. "We want to know exactly what happens to them."

"Nothing much," responded Tung, openly bored with the subject. "If they see a man they like in the other stronghold they settle down with him. If they don't, they apply to be traded again. They go on that way until they are suited. Sometimes women make me sick."

"They actually *ask* to be traded from one place to another?" questioned Grayder, surprised.

Before the other could reply the Ambassador broke in and said ponderously, "I see nothing dreadful about this, Captain. If you give your daughter away in marriage you have, in effect, traded her to the man of her choice. The chief differnce here seems to be that they won't let go of an eligible woman without receiving one in exchange."

"But——"

"And anyway it's a natural law that people marry outside their own families. A lot of intermarriage is undesirable." He eyed the subject of their questions. "You call this place of yours the Tung stronghold. Does that mean it is occupied exclusively by Tungs?"

"Yes."

"One big family? All related to each other even if distantly?"

"The Tung slaves are no relations," said the other with unconcealed contempt.

"Slaves?" chipped in Grayder, hard-eyed again. "How many slaves have the Tungs got?"

"Ten."

"How did you acquire them?"

"In a fight."

"You made prisoners of them?"

"Naturally." He seemed to view this as a singularly stupid question. "They were lying around wounded and ready for the taking. They weren't too injured to recover and get busy. Only a fool works when he can make someone else do it. We Tungs are not fools."

"How would you like it if we made a slave of *you?*" Grayder asked with much curiosity.

It took the other aback. He had a period of confusion before he replied, "Isn't that what you intend to do?"

"No."

"But I am strong and healthy. I'm more valuable alive than dead. It will be your loss if you kill me."

"We don't kill people if we can help it," Grayder told him. "Neither do we make slaves of them."

"What do you do with them?"

"Nothing."

"Then why am I here?"

"We want information. After we've got it you may go."

"You must be imbeciles," opined Alaman Tung, baffled and suspicious. "Or liars."

"Idiots and liars don't build ships like this one," Grayder retorted. "If you're up against something you can't understand don't try to understand it. Just answer our questions." He let that sink in before he went on, "How many people live in the Tung stronghold?"

"About seven hundred."

"How many other strongholds are there?"

"A lot."

"Be more specific! What number?"

"How should I know what number? How should anyone know what number?" demanded Alaman Tung. "When it is risky to stray outside one's own hunting-grounds do you expect people to explore the world? Nobody knows what number, not even the Roms."

"Roms? Who are those?"

"Dirt, fidgety dirt. They're the only ones who move around and they haven't even got a stronghold. They roam the desert like animals and every once in a while they come out and poach on somebody's hunting-grounds. They never fight if they can help it. At first sign of attack they disappear into the desert."

"Sounds like the gang we noticed using tents." ventured Major Hame.

Grayder nodded and returned to his questioning. "So you get food by hunting?"

"Mostly. The women gather some where they find it. The slaves grow some but not much."

"Wouldn't it be better, surer and easier to grow food systematically and on a wide scale?"

"What, and have it stolen in a night-raid the moment it was ready?" scoffed Alaman Tung. "We're not so witless as to grow food for others to take. Besides, it means work."

"You don't like work?"

"Who does?"

"What's wrong with it?" Grayder pressed.

"Plenty. It's stupid. It isn't necessary except for gnoits. Why work if you can live without it?"

Ignoring the point, Grayder said, "Did your father tell you that?"

"Sure he did. And his father told him. They all had brains, see? That's why you shoved our ancestors out of Terra. They had brains. You worked and they didn't. You didn't like clever people making fools of you. It advertised your inferiority for all to see. So you had to get rid of them."

"Did your father tell you that too?"

"Everybody knows it," said Tung as if stating an incontrovertible fact.

"Well," said Grayder, "if your ancestors were so remarkably superior why didn't *they* kick *us* out?"

"There were too many of you. On Terra the dopes have always outnumbered the clever."

"Am I a dope?" interjected the Ambassador curiously.

"I should think so," answered Tung. "You look one to me. I daresay that if you found something valuable belonging to somebody else you would give it back to him."

"I certainly would."

"That proves it."

A little annoyed, the Ambassador said, "And why shouldn't I give it back?"

"Finders keepers. It's the finder's reward for having his wits about him and the loser's punishment for not having them. You people seem to have no idea of common justice."

"If I stole the very clothes off your back and the food you were about to eat, would you consider it just?"

"Sure thing—if you were smart enough to do it and I was stupid enough to let you."

"You'd not take any action about it?"

"Of course I would."

"What would you do?"

"First chance I got I'd steal them back and more besides."

"Suppose there wasn't a chance?"

"Then I'd take them off some dopier dope."

"In other words," pursued the Ambassador, "you think it's every man for himself and the Devil take the hindmost?"

"It's the clever for themselves and let the stupid go soak. I don't know what you mean by the Devil. I have never heard the word."

As the Ambassador gave up, Grayder took over again and asked, "Have you ever heard of God?"

"What's that?" inquired the other blankly.

Lying back in his seat, Grayder drummed his fingers on his desk and didn't reply. He stared at Tung while his thoughts meandered around. After a while he said to the Ambassador, "To be frank, Your Excellency, I don't think this is worth continuing. We're wasting our time."

"I feel the same way about it," the Ambassador confirmed. "But Terra wants a report and expects to get one. We'd better make it look comprehensive even if it isn't. I'd like to ask this fellow a few more questions. To give him his due he is willing enough to answer."

"*If* he's doing it truthfully," commented Grayder, watching Tung.

There was no visible reaction. Without a doubt Tung had heard the remark and understood it. But he did not bristle with indignation as the average Terran would have done. He seemed completely indifferent as to whether he was viewed as a paragon of veracity or an incorrigible liar.

Grayder's own brain did a couple of somersaults as he strove to analyze the other's mind. Obviously Alaman Tung did not know the difference between right and wrong or, if he did, his estimates did not accord with Terran standards. He did not know the difference between honesty and dishonesty, justice and injustice. In view of this it was hardly likely that he could detect the wide gap between truth and untruth. If all his answers had been truthful, as was possible, it would be for one reason only, namely, that he had considered it convenient to tell the truth and inconvenient to tell lies. Expediency was the sole determining factor.

The Ambassador broke into Grayder's train of thought by asking Tung, "What method of communication is there between these various strongholds?"

"Communication?" Tung looked baffled.

"You talk with them, don't you?"

"Only in the trading season."

"Never at any other time?"

"No."

"Then how do you get news from far away?" said the Ambassador.

"We don't. What do we want news for? We can't eat it, drink it or sleep with it. What's the use of news?"

"Surely you'd like to know what's happening on your own planet?"

"We couldn't care less. We tend our own business and leave others to tend theirs," replied Tung. "What goes on elsewhere is no concern of ours. The nosey ask for all the trouble they get."

The Ambassador tried another tack. "With how many strongholds do you have contact during the trading season?"

"With all those whose hunting-grounds happen to border on ours."

"How many is that?"

"Six," said Tung.

"And the same applies to them? They have contact only with their immediate neighbors?"

"That's right."

"Are all these other strongholds the same size as yours? Do they all hold about seven hundred people?"

"The Howards have more than us, the Sommers have less but we don't know their real numbers. Somewhere there may be places twenty times the size of ours. What does it matter to us so long as they leave us alone and keep strictly to their own territory?"

"So," concluded the Ambassador, "there is no special group that maintains contact with all strongholds?"

"How could there be? They'd have to tramp over everyone's corns to get around. They wouldn't live long—unless they followed the Roms by scooting into the desert."

"Let him go," said the Ambassador to Grayder. "There is nothing more worth getting out of this character."

Grayder pressed a wall-button. The escort appeared, conducted Alaman Tung to the airlock and sent him down the ladder. Tung descended awkwardly and walked to the river with what looked like a bad limp. A canoe came in response to his yells and took him across. On the farther bank he dragged from the right leg of his pants a jungle-knife halt the size of a sword, waved it defiantly at the ship. Bidworthy, who was watching from a port, immediately held an inspection of the escort, found a trooper sans knife and defined the culprit's idiocy in a voice that resounded partway through the ship.

In the control-cabin Grayder said, "In these circumstances I can't let the men out to stretch their legs. If anyone near a stronghold is automatically regarded as an enemy it means that this world must be defined as hostile. We'd look like prize fatheads if we suffered casualties from crossbows."

"I know," replied the Ambassador. "Sergeant Gleed has been shot at already. If they didn't kill or injure him it wasn't for lack of trying." He nursed his belly in big hands while he thought over the situation. "What you are hinting is that you'd like to push straight on to the next planet, eh?"

"We'll have to go eventually, Your Excellency."

"Yes, that's true. But I think it might be wise if first we made another landing a good distance from here, picked up a second sample and cross-examined him also. We should make sure that conditions we have found right here are not peculiar to this locality. There's a slight chance they might be considerably different elsewhere. But if they're pretty much the same on the other side of the world it'll be reasonable to assume that they're the same all over."

"As you wish, Your Excellency," said Grayder, concealing his lack of enthusiasm.

"I consider it essential that our official report should give Terra the impression that we have taken some pains with it. I don't want anyone in high authority to think we merely sniffed at this planet and went away."

"No, that would be bad," Grayder agreed. He took up the intercom phone, spoke to Chief Engineer McKechnie. "Close the lock and prepare to lift."

Ten minutes afterward the warning siren wailed. Then the great ship soared in majestic silence, turned its nose over the Tung stronghold and bulleted westward. Shelton summoned Bidworthy to the cabin.

"Sergeant Major, I want you to have a squad ready in the midway lock. Immediately we land they are to hustle out and seize the first person they can lay hands on. There must be no unnecessary violence. I expect the job to be done with cool, calm efficiency. Whoever they get is to be brought straight here. Is this understood?"

"Yes, sir," snapped Bidworthy with military precision.

"This order must not, repeat *not* be treated as a pretext to smuggle a woman on board," continued Shelton, obsessed with the idea that his men were obsessed with ideas. "The captive must be an adult male, preferably with sufficient intelligence to count on his fingers. Make that quite clear to the squad, Sergeant Major."

"I certainly will, sir," promised Bidworthy, already concocting suitable phrases.

"Oh, and there is something else, Sergeant Major."

"Yes, sir?"

"I was watching through the port when that Tung fellow crossed the river. I wasn't using my field glasses but my un-aided sight is quite good. He climbed the bank and waved what appeared to be a jungle-knife, mark three, official issue, space-troops for the use of." He gave the listener his best piercing look. "Could this be possible, Sergeant Major?"

Sergeant Major admitted that it could be possible. He was sorry to add that it could also be probable. In fact it gave him much pain to describe it as practically a certainty inas-much as the presence of the knife over there had been found to coincide with the absence of one over here.

"Who lost it?" demanded Shelton with an angry snort.

"Trooper Moran, sir."

"He is remarkably well-named. How did he come to lose it?"

"He doesn't know, sir. He says first it was there and then it wasn't."

"I presume that he is reliably informed as to whether he has still got his boots on?"

"I should hope so, sir," said Bidworthy, keeping his eyes firmly focused on an invisible spot one inch in front of Shel-ton's nose.

"What have you done about this?"

Taking a long, deep breath Bidworthy gave forth like a Kevin, charged with losing equipment while on active service, tape-recorder. "1727365 Trooper Moran, Patrick Michael namely, one jungle-knife, mark three, official issue, space-troops for the use of, stores-listed at seven dollars and forty cents. Found guilty and sentenced to ten days kitchen duties, the cost of the aforesaid equipment to be deducted from his pay."

"Thank you, Sergeant Major," said Shelton, gratified.

Snapping a salute that threatened to tear off his ear, Bid-worthy removed his gaze from the invisible spot, performed an exhibitionist about-turn, crashed a steel-shod heel upon the floor and marched out.

"Discipline," commented Shelton to Grayder and the Am-bassador. "That's the thing!"

Grayder said mildly, "Maybe."

"There's no maybe about it, man. Discipline and efficiency are one and the same."

Without expression, Grayder picked up the intercom phone. "Chief, who was in charge of the airlock last time?"

"Harrison, sir."

"No, I don't want to talk to him. Just ask him if he's lost anything lately."

McKechnie went away, came back. "No, sir, nothing."

Making no remark, Grayder replaced the phone, went to the observation-port and watched the ground flowing far below. Behind him the Ambassador registered a fat smile while Shelton glowered.

The next landing was impromptu. The nose-watch spotted a hunting party returning to its stronghold, phoned the control-cabin and Grayder brought the ship down between the hunters and their destination. At once the squad of troopers rushed out, spurred on by Bidworthy's invective.

They outnumbered the quarry by two to one. Seeing this, the hunters paused not to parley but took to their heels. The fleeing ones were pretty good at it, having put in plenty of practice in the past. The result resembled a badly organized cross-country chase with the undisciplined rapidly increasing their lead over the disciplined.

Both parties swiftly diminished toward the horizon while Shelton clenched and unclenched his fists in the control-cabin and Bidworthy tramped round and round the airlock swearing horribly.

After an hour a cloud of dust appeared from a different direction, resolved itself into the hunters now leading by a couple of miles and not overstraining themselves. Stopping by the game they had dropped they picked it up, set off in a wide curve that would take them well clear of the ship and back to their stronghold.

Now the air lock phone yelped and Shelton's voice came through. "Quick, Sergeant Major! Send a fresh squad after them while they're exhausted. We've as good as got them. Put a move on, man!"

"There isn't a squad ready, sir," informed Bidworthy, sweating.

"*Make* one ready. Let's see some effective action."

Bidworthy organized a squad by the simple process of hustling out the first men he could find, regardless of their state of dress or undress. They scrambled, slid or half-fell down the ladder while frantically trying to fasten jackets, tighten belts and fix helmet-straps.

But at least they showed willing. As the dust-cloud of the first squad appeared belatedly in the distance they started off in full cry confident in the knowledge that the pursued were both tired and burdened. A long, rubber-legged corporal set the pace, bounding along like an agitated kangaroo. He covered fifty yards in record time before his pants fell down, wrapped themselves around his ankles and plunged him face-first into the dirt. The rest of the bunch hurdled him successfully except for one who paid off an old grudge by trampling on his belly.

The stronghold for which the chased were heading stood on a high bluff attainable only by one narrow path that zig-zagged up the nearest side. No river formed a barrier around it but its natural position was formidable. It resembled a tumbledown castle and was nearly twice the size of the Tung sanctuary.

Still clinging to their spoils, the hunting party reached the foot of the path and started scrambling up it as fast as they could go. By now the second squad was halfway to the bluff while the first was puffing and panting past the ship. At that point Grayder decided that enough was enough.

"I think we should sound the recall."

"Permit me to remind you," said Shelton, "that I am in charge of the troops."

"And I am in charge of the ship," said Grayder. "Do you want me to take off without them?"

"No, certainly not, but——"

"Sound the recall, Captain," suggested the Ambassador, giving Shelton no chance to argue. "After being harried all over the landscape those people will be in no mood to come here for a chat. They'll stay put and hold tight. If we want one of them we'll have to winkle him out by force."

"We're quite capable of doing that," Shelton pointed out with a trace of ire.

"I don't doubt it in the least, my dear Colonel," soothed the Ambassador. "But for heaven's sake remember that when we return to Terra any bloodshed will have to be justified to the complete satisfaction of the authorities. I do not consider that it would be justified right now. Let us try someplace else."

Shelton subsided grumpily. The ship's siren tooted three times in rapid succession. Outside the running squads skidded to a stop, looked back as if they could not credit their ears. The siren tooted again to prove that ears are worthy of credit. With visible disgust the troops mooched slowly back. Some slouched, hands in pockets, to show what they thought of brasshats who couldn't make up their minds.

Behind them the hunters ceased their hurried race up the bluff and had a wonderful time screaming highly imaginative remarks about gnoits and ponks. One who possessed a particularly shrill voice contributed several observations about snelks. Another pretended to run like mad and let his pants drop. This spectacle, plus the disorderly retreat, made Bidworthy want to climb the curtains and butter himself.

Perspiring and out of breath, the troops clambered on board while Bidworthy stood in the lock and seared each one individually. The unfortunate corporal was rewarded with an extra special doublesear. He scuttled hurriedly out of sight while Bidworthy remained glaring. With a squeak and a slam the plug wound in and the airlock closed.

Harrison said innocently, "You forgot to count their knives."

"I want no sauce from you," shouted Bidworthy. "You . . . you——"

"How about crummy snelk?" Harrison offered.

"You crummy snelk," bawled Bidworthy, too far gone to think up anything more appropriate. He stamped into the corridor and headed for the troops' quarters. The sound of his progress was like that of an elephant shod with manhole-covers.

The warning siren sounded and soon after the ship went up yet again. It covered six thousand miles before it came down and settled alongside a small lake. A stronghold occupied the whole of a rocky island in the lake's middle.

One trooper bearing a trumpet went down the ladder, advanced to the water's edge, pointed his instrument toward the island and blew the first bar of *I'm So Sad Without Mary*. Nobody had any reason to suppose that this selection approximated to what Alaman Tung had described as the trading signal. But, as Grayder had opined, in these circumstances one piece of music was as good as another and any piece was better than a long-distance race or a thump on the pate.

Most of an hour went by during which the trooper patiently sounded the call once every five minutes. Then a boat put out from the island and pulled across under three pairs of oars. It came on steadily until it was twenty yards from the shore. There it stopped.

A spokesman in the bow called in ancient accents, "Are you from Terra?"

"Yes, that's right."

"Thought so. First spaceship we've ever seen. Some folk think they're a myth. Taken you long enough to come again, hasn't it?"

"That's nothing to do with me," said the trooper, refusing to accept the responsibility. He jerked a thumb over his shoulder. "The captain would like a word with one of you."

"Would he? What's in it for us?"

"I don't know."

"Then go and ask him."

Obediently the trooper went back to the ship, phoned from the airlock. "They want to know what's in it for them, sir."

Grayder said, "Ask them what they expect."

He did so, returned and informed, "They want to know what you've got to offer."

Overhearing this, Shelton exclaimed, "The nerve of them! How about us telling them we'll sink their darned boat unless they come ashore at the double?"

"Given the free choice of all the loot on this ship," ventured the Ambassador, "it's a good bet that they'd ask for guns—assuming that they still know about Terran weapons. We can't let them have guns. This planet is listed as a penal world despite the centuries that have passed. It will remain such until the Terran authorities see fit to unlist it."

"Small arms are my department anyway," reminded Shelton. "I wouldn't donate a defective stun-gun even if they went down on their knees and begged for it."

"Nobody is thinking of giving them guns," said Grayder. He gazed thoughtfully through the port toward where the boat was lying, had a closer look through his field-glasses. The passengers, he noticed, looked even scruffiier than the Tungs. "Denims wouldn't do them any harm. They seem to have no idea of how to make decent clothes."

"Come to that, they seem to have no idea of anything that involves hard work," commented the Ambassador. "Do we have any spare denims?"

"Plenty. We're always loaded in excess of requirements." Phoning to stores, Grayder ordered a sample to be taken to the trooper. Then he switched to the airlock. "Cassidy is bringing denims to you. Take them out and show them to those mendicants. Three suits for the man who comes aboard and talks."

"Right, sir."

Watching from the control-cabin they saw the trooper march down to the beach and exhibit the bribe. Some four-sided conversation followed. Then he came back. The phone rang.

"They say they'll take the denims, sir, plus three pairs of boots like mine. They also want my trumpet."

"Holy smoke!" said Shelton, outraged. "We're dickering with the frowsy descendants of thugs like Arabs haggling over a carpet. Who do they think we are?"

"Tell them," ordered Grayder, "three suits of denims and nothing else. That's the bargain, take it or leave it."

Back traipsed the trooper. The ultimatum caused a good deal of discussion in the boat. Finally the oars dipped, the boat came to shore, one man stepped out. As the trooper led him toward the ship the other two put out their oars, retreated to what they considered a safe distance and waited.

Presently the newcomer arrived in the cabin. He had a skinny frame, the sharp, darting eyes of a wary monkey and looked rather like a racing tipster dead out of luck.

3

Grayder began the inquisition mostly because the others were content to let him.

"Sit down. What's your name?"

"Tor Hamarverd."

"What's that place on the island?"

"The Hamarverd keep."

"Keep? Don't you call it a stronghold?"

"That's a foreign word."

"Is it really? Whom do you call foreigners? Where do they live?"

"Far away over there," answered Tor Hamarverd, pointing eastward.

"Have you ever been there?"

"Not likely! One can find trouble enough without going looking for it."

"Then," said Grayder, seeking a clue to even the most rudimentary form of planetary communication, "how do you know that they use this different word?"

"We got a few foreign women by trade. They often use that word."

"Did these women permit themselves to be traded to you of their own free will?"

Hamarverd obviously viewed this question as ridiculous. "What else do you expect them to do if they don't like any man in their own keep? Don't *your* women pick and choose?"

The Ambassador interjected, "Let it pass, Captain. We've already gone over that subject. It's the same here as elsewhere and that's enough for us."

Changing the subject, Grayder eyed the other's crude attire, asked, "What do you think of the clothing we're giving you?"

"Topnotch. We could do with lots more. And some boots." He gazed hopefully at the audience. "You been sent here to fix us up with supplies?"

"No, we haven't," informed Grayder. "After all this time it's been taken for granted that you'd have got yourselves pretty well fixed up on your own account. There's been nothing to stop you that we can see. All that is needed is organization and work."

"Nobody's going to organize us," declared Hamarverd positively. "Nobody's going to make us work either. We wouldn't stand for it. To hell with them!"

The listeners exchanged glances before Grayder went on, "Seriously, have you never heard it suggested that there is virtue in work?"

"Sure have." Hamarverd let go a reminiscent chuckle. "Samel the Good he called himself. Samel the Goof was his proper name. Always prating about honesty, truthfulness and suchlike slobby stuff. Practiced what he preached, too. Worked like a slave while half the keep rode on his back. His brains were addled from birth."

"What happened to him?"

"Died of exhaustion, still yapping his stuff. He'd have lived a lot longer and easier if he hadn't been crazy."

"Nobody listened to him?"

"Only for a laugh."

"Everybody works on Terra," Grayder said.

"I can imagine."

"Don't you believe me?"

"Does *he* work?" demanded Hamarverd, pointing at the Ambassador's large paunch.

"I certainly do," assured the Ambassador.

"You look it," said Hamarverd.

"My work is extremely important, in case you don't know."

"You don't fool me, Fatski."

Grayder chipped in hurriedly. "If you doubt whether we work how d'you think we made the superior clothes we're wearing, the ship we're using?"

"You've got slaves, millions of them. And we're here because our forefathers refused to be your slaves. They chose freedom, see?"

"That is news to me," observed the Ambassador with some sarcasm.

"What is?"

"That they had any choice about coming here. To the best of my knowledge and belief they were shipped by compulsion."

"If that's the best of your knowledge, Fatski, your worst must be terrible."

"*Stop* calling me Fatski," insisted the Ambassador.

"I call you what I like," Hamarverd retorted. "You're not on Terra now."

"Neither are you, thank heavens," said the Ambassador.

Now Shelton put on his toughest expression and threatened, "If you don't see fit to be polite we won't see fit to give the promised reward."

"Don't get hard with me, you bleary-eyed ponk," said Hamarverd. "I took it for granted that the promise might not be worth the breath you'd wasted on it."

Again Grayder broke in to keep the peace. "If you doubted that you'd get the clothes why did you consent to come aboard?"

"Because we wanted to know why you'd suddenly decided to look us up after all these years."

"There are reasons of high policy."

"That's just a lot of double-talk," scoffed Tor Hamarverd. "Want me to tell you something?"

"Go ahead."

"If Terra thinks the time has come to start trading, that's all right. There are a lot of things we could do with. Right now we'll swap ten tons of fresh lizard meat for a few stutter-guns, spares and ammunition, for instance. You interested?"

"No."

"But if Terra's idea is to start some funny business you can all go and stuff yourselves. You're not going to transfer us to yet another planet. Neither are you going to walk in and confiscate this one. We're here and we're staying here, just as we are, and we're taking no lip from Terrans. You couldn't make a million of our ancestors lift a finger for you and you won't make a far larger number of us do so today."

"And who authorized you to speak for the entire world?" asked the Ambassador.

"I'm speaking for the Hamarverd keep. The other keeps can do their own talking. But it's a sure bet what they'll say." He made a gesture of contempt. "The Mullers and the Yantoffs are mentally retarded but even they aren't dopey enough to start doing chores for Terrans."

"Has it ever occurred to you," asked Grayder, "that someday you might be taken over by people who aren't remotely like Terrans?"

"Such as who?"

"Some alien lifeform with territorial ambitions."

"Such as who?" Hamarverd repeated.

"It remains to be seen," Grayder evaded.

"We'll believe it when we see it," said Hamarverd.

"By then it may be too late."

"That's our worry, not yours."

Once more Shelton interrupted. "Do you think that Terrans will sit idly by while weak, under-populated planets occupied by their blood relations are conquered one by one?"

"Who'll be doing the conquering?"

"Another lifeform, as the Captain told you."

"He told me nothing worth hearing," retorted Hamarverd. "He said that the bogey-men will get us if we don't watch out. We know who the bogey-men are!"

"Meaning Terrans, I suppose?" inquired the Ambassador.

"That's right, Fatski."

To the others the Ambassador said heavily, "This fellow's notions may or may not be representative of general opinion on this world. We haven't got the time to find out by making contact with twenty thousand or fifty thousand individual strongholds. It would take many years to do it."

"I'm afraid that that is the position, Your Excellency," agreed Grayder. "It's obvious that here we have to cope with what amounts to an enormous number of tiny, independent, self-sufficient nations each a few hundreds strong. There is no real unity among them, no central authority. Each is a law unto itself."

"We like it that way," contributed Hamarverd. "We don't like it any other way. Least of all do we like it the Terran way."

"You know little or nothing about Terra," the Ambassador pointed out. "You've been out of touch for four hundred years. Things have changed in that time."

"They're changed here too, Fatski."

"Not for the better that I can see. You appear to have established a stupid, inefficient compromise between the family unit and the old-style gang system. The result is a lot of petty clans each with its jerry-built headquarters, its hunting grounds and nothing else. No comfort, no security, no progress, no morals."

"No taxes, no work, no regimentation," Hamarverd added.

The Ambassador dismissed this with a disdainful wave of

his hand. "Let him have those denims. He needs them, God knows. Doubtless he'd appreciate a few bars of soap as well."

Hamarverd said suspiciously, "What's soap?"

"Stuff that gets rid of the smell."

"What smell?"

"You wouldn't know, having lived with it so long," said the Ambassador. "But I've a pretty good idea of why your women get themselves traded from place to place. Hope springs eternal in the human breast."

Scowling, Hamarverd asked, "Are you trying to be funny, you pot-bellied slob?"

"That's enough!" interjected Grayder, sharply. He turned and addressed the trooper who had just entered. "Give him the denims and let him go."

"Right, sir!"

The two departed. Soon afterward Hamarverd went to the shore bearing a bundle under one arm. The boat pulled in, took him aboard. Then it edged away for fifty yards and stopped there, rocking gently in the calm water, while its three occupants shouted unhearable remarks and made vulgar gestures at the ship.

Picking up the phone, Shelton said, "Ah, Sergeant Major, has Trooper Wagstaff got his knife?"

There was a short silence before Bidworthy came back with, "Yes, sir."

"Well, that's something," said Shelton.

Gazing through the port at the rude antics of those in the boat, the Ambassador said with much sourness, "A world full of no-good bums."

"Hereditary or environmental?" prompted Grayder.

"Obviously hereditary. Don't you think so?"

"I'm far from sure, Your Excellency."

"Not sure?" The Ambassador stared at him. "Originally we shipped a million hardened criminals, didn't we?"

"Yes, that's right."

"And what have we seen here?"

"I don't know. The characters we threw out of Terra were multiple murderers, incorrigible perverts, all the criminal rubbish we could well afford to lose. Their descendants don't seem quite as bad as that. I'll readily admit they're off their heads in some respects but that doesn't make them criminals in the same sense that their forefathers were."

"Sorry, I don't agree with you, Captain," curtly responded the Ambassador. "They're dirty, dissolute, lazy, shiftless and totally without moral fiber. They are criminals suffering from serious lack of opportunity to be criminals—because in a world composed solely of their own kind, dog can only eat dog."

"The real test would come," offered Shelton, "if we transferred some of them back to Terra."

"Heaven forbid!" said the Ambassador. He took a chair, lay back and pondered awhile before he went on, "On each world I am supposed to make contact with the central authority and come to an agreement about mutual defense. Being listed as hostile, this world is the only exception. Here, I am expected to use my own judgment in the light of existing conditions."

He eyed the others as if inviting comment, but none came. So he continued, "I am also supposed to establish myself as the representative of Terran authority on the biggest, best-organized world, leaving a Consul complete with staff and bodyguard on each of the others."

"Fat lot of use that would be here," opined Colonel Shelton. "You'd need a vertible army of bureaucrats even if you appointed only one per stronghold. Moreover, to live beyond a week, each would need a bodyguard large enough to protect him morning, noon and night." He paused to let it sink in, finished, "Estimate the total number of troops required and you'll find it amounts to complete military occupation of the planet."

"Unthinkable!" declared the Ambassador. "The strategic value is too low and the cost too high." He did a bit more thinking, decided, "Before we can get anywhere with this planet it will have to undergo extensive and intensive education and organization, whether it likes it or not. That is Terra's problem and not ours. We'll make out a comprehensive report for the benefit of the experts and——"

He was cut off by the sound of a tremendous raspberry blown somewhere outside. Grayder went to the port and looked out expectantly. So did the others.

The boat was now halfway across the lake and progressing slowly toward the island keep. A figure stood in its bow holding something that had a metallic glitter. Again came the derisive sound. Reaching for his field-glasses, Grayder looked through them, silently handed them to Shelton. He in turn had a look, let go an oath and grabbed the telephone.

"Is Sergeant Major Bidworthy there? Then where is he? Well go and fetch him. I wish to speak to him immediately."

At the other end a voice called, "Hey, Casartelli, the Colonel wants the S.M."

Beyond it another voice echoed hollowly along a metal corridor, "Hey, Pongo, you there? Old Cheeseface is howling for Ruthless Rufus. You tell him."

Shelton growled into the phone, "Kindly inform Trooper Casartelli that he will report to Old Cheeseface in one hour's time."

"Yes, sir," came back in startled tones. Then, after a pause, "The Sergeant Major is coming right now, sir."

"Well, Sergeant Major?" inquired Shelton grimly when Bidworthy was on the line.

There sounded an embarrassed cough before Bidworthy said in precise, formal tones, "I regret to report, sir, that Trooper Wagstaff has lost his trumpet."

"And how did he contrive to do that?"

"He left it upon a rock on the shore, sir, while he conducted that visitor to the ship. Since he did not take the visitor back to the shore he forgot the trumpet. He has only just remembered it."

"Because those louts in the boat have seen fit to remind him," said Shelton sarcastically.

Another long-drawn and somewhat over-ripe noise came across the waters by way of confirmation. Shelton looked pained.

"I take a very poor view of this, Sergeant Major."

"Yes, sir."

"It was our only trumpet."

"Yes, sir."

"We are issued with one and no more."

"Yes, sir."

"And now it has gone."

"Yes, sir."

"That and a jungle-knife."

"Yes, sir."

"Can't you say anything else but 'Yes, sir'?" shouted Shelton.

"Yes, sir," Bidworthy admitted.

"Then say it!"

Sucking in a good, long breath, Bidworthy let go with, "1768421 Trooper Wagstaff, Arnold Edward Sebastian, charged with losing equipment while on active service, namely, one B-flat Gabriel Horn, brass——"

"One *what?*" asked Shelton.

"One B-flat Gabriel Horn," repeated Bidworthy. "It is the correct stores definition, sir."

"I don't want to hear any more," said Shelton, and slammed down the phone. Angrily he stamped out of the cabin.

Raising his eyebrows, the Ambassador remarked, "Our dear Colonel appears to be irked."

"We all have our bad moments," said Grayder.

"True, true." The Ambassador released a deep sigh. "We have other worlds yet to visit. Do you think that we can manage without a trumpet?"

"I should hope so, Your Excellency."

"Then what is eating Shelton?"

The ship went up but did not immediately depart. It circumnavigated the planet a couple of times and took photographs to add to those made during the first approach. This record covered only a few well-selected portions of the sunlit side but provided a fair sampling of the world as a whole.

A photographic interpretation squad got busy with these pictures and concocted some data based upon the known size and population of the Tung stronghold. As the ship raced through the starfield they produced their statistics.

The world as a whole, they said, probably contained about sixteen thousand strongholds, not counting fifty or a hundred Rom encampments. The strongholds ranged in size from small ones of four hundred inhabitants to the largest with three thousand, the average probably being about twelve hundred. The world's total population was probably between seventeen and eighteen millions.

Reading through this report, the Ambassador said ironically, "I find this most useful. It justifies the expert time spent upon it. We now have a number of so-called facts each preceded by the word 'probably.' It shows commendable caution on the part of those who don't want to accept responsibility for their own statements."

"An intelligent guess is better than no guess at all, Your Excellency," suggested Shelton, who by now had worked off his ire on the unfortunate Trooper Casartelli.

"It isn't even an intelligent guess," denied the Ambassador. "It is based solely upon what can be seen. No account has been taken of what cannot be seen."

"I don't know how it is possible to do that," said Shelton, failing to understand what the other was getting at.

"I neither ask nor expect the impossible," the Ambassador gave back. "My point is that data based exclusively on the visible may be made completely worthless by the invisible." He tapped the report with an authoritative forefinger. "They estimate sixteen thousand strongholds—above ground. How many are below ground?"

"Subterranean ones?" exclaimed Shelton, startled.

"Of course. There may be fifty thousand of those for all we know."

"We didn't see any."

"He says we didn't see any," the Ambassador said to Grayder. He spread hands to indicate that there was no comment worth making.

Grayder observed, "There were other things we didn't see."

"I know," answered the Ambassador. "We didn't see any women, not one. But since the race exists it's reasonable to assume that its females exist. That's an intelligent guess made independently of visible evidence."

"They mentioned their women repeatedly," Shelton pointed out.

Ignoring that, the Ambassador went on, "We have soared over more strongholds than I'd care to count without seeing a single factory. However, I don't think they've those hidden underground. It is my opinion that they have no factories—they have too low a standard of living and too strong a dislike of honest work."

"There's something else they don't seem to have," contributed Grayder. He mused a moment, said, "The crooks we deported were, I believe, a drunken lot. About ninety percent of them were incurable alcoholics."

"So——?" prompted the Ambassador.

"We haven't seen anything resembling a brewery or a distillery."

"Come to that, we haven't," the Ambassador admitted.

"Which means," finished Grayder, "that no matter what other faults they may have the present inhabitants are at least a sober crowd."

"Not necessarily. They may lack the raw materials necessary for large-scale brewing. Or the technique, the know-how. So they've turned to native drugs. That Tor Hamarverd was glassy-eyed, insulting and aggressive. A hophead if ever I saw one."

Grayder shrugged, not wishing to argue the point. Discussion was futile, anyway. For sheer lack of facts the subject must remain speculative and the injection of personal prejudices didn't help one little bit. Fatski naturally resented having been called Fatski and that made the name-caller a drug-addict.

"When I was a kid," informed the Ambassador, "I detested

spinach. Whenever I found it on my plate I bolted it first. Then, having got rid of it, I could proceed to enjoy my dinner." He smiled at the memory. "That is what we've done: we've disposed of the only hostile planet and now should have something more pleasant in prospect. Which is the next one, Captain?"

"A place said to be named Hygeia."

"Oh, yes, I remember now that it was second on the list. I was supposed to read up what little is known about these dumps but never found the time. What information have you got in that little book of yours?"

"Not much. Hygeia is recorded as a warm, lush and fertile world that was confiscated by a crowd who called themselves the Sons of Freedom. They went away, shipload by shipload, until there were none left on Terra. Some time latter another and different lot, known as Naturists, also went to Hygeia, presumably with the consent of the first ones. The grand total of those who scooted is not known but is thought to be about two and a half millions."

"Sons of Freedom," cogitated the Ambassador. "Weren't they a religious sect better known as Quakers?"

"No, Your Excellency. You are thinking of the Society of Friends. They took over a planet which they named Amity. It isn't on our list for this trip. Maybe some other expedition is looking them up."

"In which case they'll be dead out of luck," put in Shelton. "I read about them once and have good reason to remember them. Stiff-necked pacifists, every one."

"What do we care?" asked the Ambassador. "Let them be somebody else's grief."

"This other mob may be just as bad," Shelton offered. "I've never heard of the Sons of Freedom but it sounds anarchistic to me."

"Know anything about them, Captain?" the Ambassador asked.

"No, Your Excellency. More than three hundred minorities took flight during the years of the Great Explosion. One cannot remember the full details of all of them."

"I suppose not. We could do with a professor of history on board." He contemplated the wall in meditative silence, then said, "One thing is sure—they'll be crackpots. But it can be said that crackpots are a few cuts above common criminals."

"Provided they keep their thieving fingers to themselves," topped Shelton. "I have an idea that the moment all these isolated groups set greedy eyes on a ship loaded with stuff they need they'll immediately believe in Santa Claus."

"Well, you've got one worry off your mind," the Ambassador told him. "They cannot steal a trumpet."

The next world bloomed out of space like a brilliant blue-green ball that circled a pale orange sun closely resembling Sol. Nine other planets and a dozen satellites completed this system but according to ancient reports Hygeia was the only one inhabited.

Cameras started snapping the day-side as soon as the planet had swelled sufficiently for its surface details to be revealed. Vast areas of forest stood untouched, many rivers flowed without a bridge across them. A considerable portion of the land area remained undeveloped and perhaps unexplored.

All the same, the occupied part of the territory showed that the settlers had done well for themselves. Highways and railroad tracks ran through many of the broadest, most fertile valleys which were intensively cultivated to the very edge of the forests. Through these valleys, villages and towns were strung like beads. Here and there small factories could be seen, also several quarries and opencast mining sites. There was a waterside city with a dockyard system in which white-sailed ships were lying at rest.

The general impression was of a population several times larger and considerably more energetic than that of the previous world. These visible results formed an object lesson for the lazy and proved yet again that by the sweat of thy brow shalt thou achieve something or other.

For his landing Grayder picked a long, low ridge with a granite outcrop. He was not interested in choosing the best position from the strategic viewpoint; the tonnage he was handling demanded a resting-place of solid bedrock and it was his responsibility to put the ship down someplace where it would not bury itself up to the airlock doors.

The vessel settled with the usual creaking and cracking sounds beneath the keel. Power cut off. Air-vents gaped and sucked in fresh atmosphere, warm and rich with oxygen. The fore, aft and midway airlocks were opened. This time the crew did not drop a ladder: they lowered the gangways.

Emergence was in strict order of precedence. First the Ambassador who planted an august foot on the world with the air of saying, "I claim this planet in the name of Terra." Second came Captain Grayder, informal and impassive. Third, Colonel Shelton, frowning around as if hoping for the best but expecting the worst. Fourth, the senior civil servant, peering curiously through thick-lensed glasses.

Then, of course, the next grade lower and in the same order: His Excellency's private secretary, the ship's second officer, Major Hame, second in command of troops, the penultimate pen-pusher.

Down another grade and then another until there was left only His Excellency's barber, boot-wiper and valet, crew-members with the lowly status of O.S.—Ordinary Spaceman—troopers with the lowlier status of plain, nondescript troopers, and a number of temporary ink-pots dreaming of the day when they would be made permanent and given desks of their own. This last collection of unfortunates remained aboard to clean ship and refrain from smoking, by command.

Had the world been alien, hostile and well-armed the order of exit would have been reversed, thus exemplifying the Biblical promise that the last shall be first and the first shall be last. But this planet, though officially new, unofficially was not new and certainly not alien. As for its total lack of hostility, that was taken for granted. The Hygeians were not criminals and therefore could be trusted to show proper respect for their betters.

From the foot of the ridge stretched fields bearing a heavy crop of what resembled barley. A gentle wind sent shadows racing through the grain like waves upon a sea. On one side the cultivation ended where the forest began at the rim of the horizon. To the other side, a mile away, stood a medium-sized town.

Through field-glasses they examined the town. Suburban houses, which were nearest, proved small but attractive and seemed solidly built in brick or stone. No tall buildings arose from the center, the highest having only four floors. The whole place basked in clean air and bright sunshine with no haze or smog above its rooftops. Of mechanical road vehicles there wasn't a sign but from the northern outskirts trailed a long, fluffy line of vapor where a steam-locomotive headed away.

"Well, my dear Captain," enthused the Ambassador, "I must say that this looks lots better than did the last dump." Approvingly he sniffed the invigorating air. "A most attractive place and a worthy addition to our empire."

"Yes, Your Excellency," said Grayder, not bothering to suggest that the inhabitants might have different ideas.

"I'd like it better," put in Shelton, "if they had more manpower and greater industrial potential. Militarily speaking, they are weak. A mutual defense pact will be a one-sided bargain so far as we are concerned."

"No addition to Terran strength is to be despised," contradicted the Ambassador. "Besides, these faraway planets will serve as buffer states and absorb the first blows."

Grayder felt tempted to ask, "From whom?" but held his peace. Within the last few centuries Blieder ships had probed a considerable piece of the cosmos without finding any form of life more intelligent than an Earth-dog. To his mind, all this glib talk about a prospective menace from space was nothing but a pretext to extend authority as far as it could be taken.

Peering through his field-glasses again, the Ambassador said with satisfaction, "Well, the problem of making contact is about to be solved. A couple of people are coming to us through the barley." He registered a gratified smile. "Nice of them to react so promptly."

"It could also be stupid of them," opined Shelton. "How do they know that this is a Terran ship? If they had no more sense than the average hick—which isn't saying much—they'd scout around and make sure of our identity before approaching us."

Still watching the oncomers, of whom nothing could be seen save two heads above the waving grain, the Ambassador replied, "They must have been working nearby when we came down, otherwise they could not have appeared so soon. That means they are agricultural workers. You cannot expect a pair of farmhands to be military geniuses, my dear Colonel."

Shelton subsided, still thinking that wariness was not too much to ask of anyone, even a hayseed. The group continued to watch while the others made their way carefully through the grain and eventually emerged at the foot of the ridge. Now they started climbing toward the ship.

At that point the Ambassador drooped his field-glasses, rubbed his eyes and blinked several times. Shelton emitted an outraged grunt. Behind him, Sergeant Major Bidworthy rumbled like an active volcano.

4

The Hygeians were very tall, well-built to the point of being over-muscled. Each carried a personal bag slung by a strap from one shoulder. Each was tastefully attired in a pair of sandals, those and nothing more. Apart from the foot gear they were as naked as on the day they were born.

Studying his audience with unconcealed disdain, one gave fraternal greeting by saying, "Terrans—as dirty-minded as ever."

The Ambassador was taking a second look when this observation hit him over the head. He bristled at once.

"What d'you mean?"

"Hiding yourselves from the glorious sunshine and the face of creation," informed the other. Letting his gaze linger significantly upon the ambassadorial belly, he remarked to his companion, "I suppose it can be conceded that this one has good reason to be ashamed of his body, eh, Pincuff?"

"Yaz," agreed Pincuff. "Years of greed and neglect have taken their toll."

"I resent that," said the Ambassador.

"He resents it, Boogle," said Pincuff. Then he let go a loud and vulgar laugh. His roving eyes took in the ship, found its ports full of astonished faces. "Look at that lot, Boogle. Afraid to come out and show themselves. Pale and weedy to a man."

"Yaz," Boogle confirmed. "God bless their shrivelled little chests." Then he threw himself flat, did twenty push-ups, sprang to his feet and massaged his bare midriff. "Let's see you do *that*," he invited the Ambassador.

"For your information, I am the Terran representative and not a circus acrobat."

"You don't say? Then how about doing a mere six up-and-downs?"

"No. Certainly not."

"Just one then," pleaded Boogle. "One for a start. You can always work up to more. Do you a lot of good."

"I am the sole arbiter of what does me good," declared the Ambassador, holding his temper grimly in check. "And I have not come here to indulge in pointless calisthenics. I wish to meet someone in a position of authority."

"What for?"

"The purpose is confidential."

"Hear that?" Boogle asked Pincuff, full of suspicion. "There's something smelly here."

"It' coming from the ship," Pincuff informed. "Full of stale air and old clothing. Nobody has bathed for months. A real goat's nest."

"The ship air is automatically cleaned and sterilized six times per hour," Grayder told him.

"I should think so, too," approved Pincuff. "Else you could cut it with a knife."

"Real stinkers," Boogle added for good measure. "Probably the only form of life that has found it necessary to invent delousing stations."

"And where did you hear about those?" asked the Ambassador coldly.

"We've been educated. We know a lot concerning Terra. Everyone there is dirty-minded about his own body, dirty in physique, dirty in habits. Diseased, verminous and depraved. Persecutors of anyone who isn't afraid to face the wind, the rain and the sun in his natural state."

"You call that education?"

"Yaz. And it is, too."

Changing his angle of attack, the Ambassador hazarded, "I suppose these are the orthodox teachings of the Sons of Freedom, eh?"

"Jumping Joseph!" exclaimed Pincuff, horrified. "He thinks we're Doukhobors."

"If you want the Douks," said Boogle contemptuously, "they're way over the hills playing around in the mud. We drove them out a couple of hundred years ago."

"Why?"

"Couldn't get on with them no matter how we tried. A preaching, praying, mealy-mouthed bunch always trying to convert us to their way of thinking and abusing us when we refused to see the light. They thought that because we Naturists had been victimized for nakedness we must be easy meat. They let us come here with the idea of boosting their own strength. That was their mistake."

"And what happened?"

"We bided our time until we were ready and then we rushed them down south. Anyone who joins the Douks is mentally deficient. And that's one thing we Naturists are not." He performed a couple of full stretches, danced around and shadowboxed for half a minute, finished with, "A healthy mind in a healthy body. Do I speak wisdom, Pincuff?"

"Yaz," said Pincuff.

The Ambassador fished for information. "Do you people outnumber these . . . er . . . Douks?"

"Sure do. By at least twenty to one. They're dying out."

"Which means that Naturists hold most of the developed part of the planet?"

"Correct."

"So that to all intents and purposes your government is the government of this world?"

"Yaz."

"Good! I want to have an interview with members of the government."

"He doesn't want much," observed Pincuff, speaking to nobody in particular.

"Sure doesn't," confirmed Boogle. "Go fetch me your government—just like that. Thinks they're sitting around waiting for us to summon them and they'll come on the run."

"Flatterer," said Pincuff to the Ambassador.

"All I ask," the Ambasador persisted, "is that you go to that town and report our presence. Officialdom can be trusted to do something about it."

"The town is well aware of your presence," Pincuff assured. "It's within plain view and they can't have failed to notice the landing of a ship this size."

"We've got eyes," contributed Boogle. "Good healthy ones." He pointed to the senior civil servant who was staring at him fascinatedly through horn-rimmed spectacles. "We're not half-blind like that dumb-looking wreck."

"Bet you fifty percent of them wear glasses," said Pincuff. "And half of those who don't are in need of them."

"Same with false teeth," supported Boogle. He gaped wide open, revealing a double row of pure white fangs, and shoved this spectacle towards the Ambassador's face. "All my own. How many have *you* got?"

"That is nothing to do with you," said the Ambassador.

"Won't talk," Boogle told the general assembly. "Not a real tooth in his head."

"But arch supports in his boots," guessed Pincuff.

"I do not use arch supports," the Ambassador denied.

"Then let's see you do this." Boogle bounced up and down like a demented kangaroo. "Go ahead and try it. Keep time with me. One-sy, two-sy, I'll beat you-sy. Two-sy, three-sy, you beat me-sy."

"Nonsense!" said the Ambassador flatly.

"Physical fitness is nonsense," Boogle informed Pincuff. "Can you imagine anything more typically Terran?"

"Yaz," said Pincuff. "Dirty-mindedness."

The Ambassador turned to Grayder, Shelton and the others. "No useful purpose can be served by prolonging this stupid conversation. Let us go into the ship and wait until someone with more brains arrives."

With that he marched up the gangway. The rest followed, carefully maintaining the proper order of precedence. Bidworthy went last, pausing only to sear the Hygeians with his glare.

"Defective liver and superfluous bile," diagnosed Pincuff.

"Fatty buttocks," added Boogle. "Hopelessly out of condition. Needs a twenty-mile race and an hour in the steambath."

"You two can go to hell," declared Bidworthy and made the gangway tremble with the thunder of his ascent.

"Foul-mouthed as well," remarked Pincuff as if confirming a foregone conclusion. "Let's get back to civilization."

Ignoring the hundreds of faces still gaping from the ports, they turned and headed toward the town, perforce showing the audience their hinder parts. To the onlookers this rear-end view held vague suggestion of a declaration of independence.

First Mate Morgan peered into the cubby-hole, frowned at what he saw. "What, are you at it again? Can't you think of any better way in which to spend your spare time?"

"Yes—riding around," answered Tenth Engineer Harrison. "I can't do that in the ship. I've got to be outside with a firm road under my wheels and a pleasant landscape before me. You don't mind me tending to my bike, do you?"

"I couldn't care less," said Morgan. "But I still think it a crazy way to use one's off-duty." Producing a notebook, he poised a pencil over it. "Which leave roster d'you want to be on, first, second or third?"

"So we're getting leave, are we?"

"Not immediately. Our entitlement starts at six o'clock Thursday evening. The Captain knows the regulations and he'll expect me to produce the rosters for his approval. Which one d'you want to be on?"

"There are advantages and disadvantages," mused Harrison, rubbing his nose with a polishing-cloth. "The first bunch go out blind whereas the last have the benefit of information brought back by the earlier ones. On the other hand, if the first lot arouse the dislike of the natives the last lot will have to bear the brunt of it. A couple of rowdy drunks can earn later comers a harvest of black eyes."

"Make up your mind," urged Morgan impatiently. "I can't stand here all day while you examine the respective merits of this, that and the other. Which d'you want, first, second or third?"

"I'll take third. I'd rather go out primed than ignorant."

"Third," repeated Morgan, writing it down. "Where are Ninth Engineer Hope and Eighth Engineer Carslake?"

"Went running to their cabins a couple of minutes ago. Said they wanted to load their cine-cameras. They seemed to be excited about something."

"Did they?" Morgan eyed him briefly. "Where have you been this last hour?"

"Right here, cleaning my bike. Why? Anything wrong with that?"

"No, nothing wrong." Morgan went in search of Hope and Carslake, leaving the other staring after him.

A little later Harrison was spinning his rear wheel and listening to the smooth, oily ticking of its ball-race when Sergeant Gleed looked in.

"Morgan been after you yet?"

"Yes."

"What did you pick?"

"Third roster."

"A mistake," pronounced Gleed. "Leave won't last that long. You should have chosen to go first. A bird in the hand is worth two on the bust."

"In the bush," corrected Harrison.

"You know what I mean. Rush to open when opportunity knocks and pause not for cogitation. The first bunch will get away with murder. The second might. The third won't."

"Why not?"

"There'll be trouble aplenty with at least some of the first crowd. You know what sailors are."

"What d'you mean?"

"The local warriors are going to object to the way some of our fellows use their eyes. One thing will lead to another as sure as Bidworthy barks in his sleep. It'll end up in a real free-for-all if not a massacre. Grayder will then refuse to approve the next roster."

"Don't know what you're so morbid about," observed Harrison, starting to give his saddle its sixth successive polish. "There's no reason why we should find more trouble here than in any other place."

"How long have you been fooling around with this contraption?"

"I don't know. I don't time myself. I'm not on duty so what does it matter?"

"You've not had a look at the natives?"

"No," said Harrison. "They're our own kind, exactly the same as ourselves. I've seen Terrans aplenty."

"Not stark," said Gleed.

"What d'you mean, stark?"

"These Hygeians are stark raw."

"I don't understand."

"How about treating yourself to a lucid moment?" Gleed suggested, and went on, "They're naked. Not a stitch."

"Oh, no!"

"Oh, yes!" insisted Gleed.

"Women as well?"

"We've seen none as yet but you can bet on it."

"I don't believe it."

"You will," promised Gleed.

Towards eventide a deputation arrived. It consisted of half a dozen elderly, sunburnt nudists led by one who looked ninety years older than God. This character sported a thirty-inch beard that concealed his chest and much of his abdomen and gave him the appearance of being improperly dressed. He was carrying a gold-painted rod bearing on its top a wooden disc carved with what resembled a coat of arms.

Reaching the foot of the gangway, the bearded one gazed up at the airlock doorway in which Sergeant Gleed was lounging. A brief look of distaste passed across his aged features before he lifted his rod ceremoniously and spoke.

"Health be yours."

"It is," said Gleed, not feeling especially decrepit.

The other seemed to doubt this assurance but was not inclined to dispute it. "I am Radaschwon Bouchaine, the mayor of Sunnyside." He gestured toward the town. Then he indicated his fellows who were studying Gleed's clothing with the air of maiden ladies inspecting a long-dead rat. "And these are some of my councillors."

"How nice," acknowledged Gleed, rewarding them with a craggy smile.

"We would like to meet your leader," finished Mayor Bouchaine.

"Wait there and I'll see what he says." Gleed took the intercom phone from the wall, listened to its steady buzz-buzz at the other end, decided that so far as he was concerned whoever answered would be the leader. As it happened it was Grayder. To him, Gleed said, "There's a bunch of nakes at the gangway, sir, and they want to have a word with you. One of them says he's the local mayor. He's got a totem-pole to prove it."

"Bring them to the chartroom, Sergeant," ordered Grayder.

Gleed returned to the top of the gangway. "You can come aboard."

That started an argument among the seven during which the words dirt, germs and vermin were freely used. Gleed listened with growing ire, not liking their ready acceptance of the notion that everyone on the ship was crammed to the ears with bacteria.

Eventually he gave way to his feelings and bawled, "What d'you think this is, a leper colony?"

A momentary silence fell before Mayor Bouchaine asked, "Couldn't your leader come to see us out here?"

"No, Pop. I don't give him orders. He gives them to me. He's just told me to bring you to the chartroom. Are you coming or not?"

"At my age what have I to lose?" remarked the Mayor, commencing to climb the gangway. Five of the councillors reluctantly followed. The sixth sat down on his hams and assumed the expression of a determined non-starter.

"Mayor, I'm not prepared to accept the risk of contamination."

"You do as you please, Gerpongo," said the Mayor, going up.

"You do as you please, Gerpongo," echoed Gleed as unpleasantly as possible. "You squat on your fundament, Gerpongo, and be happy. Let the fresh, clean air play around your chassis, Gerpongo, and you'll be topnotch."

"That ought everyone to do," said Gerpongo pointedly. "And that is my intention."

Somewhat disgruntled, Gleed led the way through the ship, the others padding after him in single file. He noticed that they maintained complete silence, exchanging no remarks, and got the idea that they were trying to avoid breathing any more than was absolutely necessary. Reaching the chartroom, he showed them inside and went away muttering to himself.

"Gerpongo," he said. It sounded like an alien cuss-word.

Within the room the Mayor stroked his beard and looked in turn at the Ambassador, Captain Grayder, Colonel Shelton and Major Hame, decided to address himself to the former.

"Health be yours."

"Thank you," said the Ambasssador, relishing a fragment of courtesy.

"This is the first ship to come here from the old world since we became established," the Mayor went on. "Naturally we have taken it for granted that Terra isn't interested in us. We've had every reason to do so. But now it seems that we were wrong. The government has told me to seek an interview and ask the purpose of this visit."

"Oh, so you have been in touch with your government already?"

"Of course. I phoned through to Radiant City immediately you landed."

"Well, now," said the Ambassador, highly pleased, "it would simplify matters if we could deal direct with your chief officials." He turned to Grayder. "The pictures, Captain." From a drawer Grayder extracted the enormously enlarged photographs and spread them on his desk. The Ambassador suggested to Mayor Bouchaine, "Now if you will be so good as to show us the precise location of Radiant City we'll move the ship there and thus save you a lot of time and trouble."

"You mean you want me to point to our seat of government?"

"That's right."

"I am not authorized to do so."

The Ambassador eyed him with surprise. "Why not?"

"I shall have to consult them first," insisted the Mayor.

"But why on earth shouldn't you tell us where your government is? What possible harm can it do? You don't think we're scheming to overthrow it, do you?"

"I cannot accept the responsibility of transferring a potential epidemic to our capital," said the Mayor flatly.

"An epidemic?" The Ambassador gazed bewilderedly around the room. "An epidemic of what?"

"We want no Terran diseases here," the Mayor informed. "If a center of infection is positioned adjacent to Radiant City it must be with official permission."

"Frankly, I can't imagine what you're talking about," exclaimed the Ambassador. "After all, you people are of Terran origin and therefore it follows that any sickness you may have must also be Terran."

"We don't have illnesses apart from the common cold," said the Mayor.

"And lumbago," contributed a councillor.

"And an occasional bellyache," offered another, then hurriedly added, "Attributable to a mistake in diet. People should not make such errors. If they do they must expect to suffer. Diet is very important."

"That's right, Rampot," approved a third. "A healthy mind in a healthy body."

"Look," chipped in the Ambassador, "I want to come to an understanding with your government."

"About what?" inquired the Mayor, fingering his beard and looking foxey.

"About making a military agreement."

"Military?" Mayor Bouchaine screwed up his eyes until they almost disappeared. He had a period of strenuous thought before he admitted, "I've come across that word somewhere, probably in our history books. But for the life of me I can't remember what it means?"

"So you have no army, no soldiers?"

"Army? Soldiers?"

"No warriors, no fighters?"

"Ah, yaz, fighters." The Mayor's whiskery face showed sudden understanding. "We have boxers and wrestlers in great number. Strong, athletic and highly skilled, I assure you. I once saw one throw four Douks into the river and did they get wet! Let me tell you——"

Colonel Shelton, who had been listening with incredulity, interrupted by asking, "When you chased out the Doukhobors did you ever *kill* one?"

"Hear that?" the Mayor said to his councillors who were mutually appalled. He looked around as if seeking somewhere to vomit.

"Well, what *did* you do to them?" persisted Shelton.

"We smacked their bottoms," informed the Mayor as though mentioning the obvious.

Openly disgusted, Shelton said, "What would you do if attacked by a lifeform so alien and bizarre that you couldn't tell its bottom from its top?"

"Which lifeform is that?"

"One that may come upon you suddenly and without warning."

"From where?"

"From anywhere out of the cosmos."

"Faulty diet and unhealthy living creates bad dreams," remarked the Mayor virtuously. "We never have bad dreams."

"It'll be more than a bad dream when it really happens," Shelton persisted.

"It hasn't happened in the last four hundred years and we've no reason to suppose it will happen in the next four thousand."

"You're in poor position to do any supposing," Shelton pointed out. "You've no ships, you're doing no cosmic exploration. You're just sitting around in yours skins and waiting for the blow to fall."

"That's right," chimed in the Ambassador for good measure. "There might have been a non-human people native to this planet; it'd have been wholly their own fault if they'd been taken by surprise when you poured in from Terra. Surely you can see that what you have done others can do equally as well? If another intelligence should suddenly expand into the starfield and take a liking to Hygeia——"

The Mayor thought it over. "Yaz, that is true. What we have done somebody else could do—if there is a somebody else to do it. But it is not for me to consider such a hypothetical problem. I'll pass it along to our government."

"Good!" said the Ambassador.

"But," continued Mayor Bouchaine, "they will want to know what all this has to do with Terra. What am I to say?"

"Tell them that a ruthless enemy could swiftly conquer a few weak, independent worlds one at a time. It would be a vastly different matter to take on a powerful confederation, in close communication, united in resolve to beat off the common foe. So Terra thinks it high time steps were taken to reach a mutual understanding."

"What steps?"

"Just for a start," informed the Ambassador as glibly as possible, "we would like to establish a consul upon Hygeia. He would function as our representative, a mere token of Terran authority. Of course we'd have to provide him with a small staff to deal with routine matters. And a bodyguard."

"A bodyguard? What for?"

"To protect him against outside attack. Such protection is his entitlement and our responsibility, you understand?

Just a company of forty or fifty troops armed with modern weapons. They'd be quite an asset to your own defences, too." He bestowed a smile of pure benevolence. "We'd also like to leave a couple of powerful long-range transmitters with enough technicians to keep them in operation."

"Putting us in permanent contact with Terra?" suggested the Mayor, hinting at a skunk in the bed.

"Yes, of course. Swift communication is essential in space-war. How can we rush to your aid unless we know that you need it?"

"I don't know," admitted the Mayor, unable to find a satisfactory answer but convinced that he was seeing the thin end of the wedge. "I'll phone through to headquarters. It's up to them to make the decisions."

"You do that," approved the Ambassador.

Gleed conducted them through the airlock, watched them go down the gangway. Gerpongo got off his hams, fumbled in his shoulder-bag, produced a thing resembling a fire-extinguisher. The others stood in line and held their jaws wide open while Gerpongo sprayed each in turn. He made a thorough job of it, tending first to their mouths and then to their bodies, front and back. An odor faintly reminiscent of coal-tar and cinnamon drifted up to the airlock. First Mate Morgan joined Gleed as that worthy snorted his disgust.

"So the conflab is finished?" said Morgan.

"Yes. They're now busy killing brasshat lice or something. Don't want to go home with Terran passengers in their hair."

"If the Captain is disengaged I'd better see him about this first roster. You're on it, aren't you?"

"I am. But I don't know whether it's worth it."

"Not worth getting away from this metal can for a few hours? Not worth treading good, solid earth, going to town, seeing the bright lights and having a wonderful time? Are you sickening for something?"

"I'm suspicious," said Gleed.

"Of what?"

"That everyone in that place will carefully keep their distance. And that if anyone does speak to us he or she will do so from ten yards away while fanning the air towards us."

"Then fan it back," advised Morgan. "The answer to an implied smell is an imaginary stench."

"Some spree, eh?" said Gleed. "The pinnacle of gay abandon. Everyone wafting the atmosphere at everyone else. Man, the prospect thrills me so that I can hardly wait."

"It'd be exercise if nothing else," opined Morgan. "I'm going to see Grayder." Leaving the airlock, he trudged along corridors, reached the chartroom, knocked and entered. He laid a paper on the Captain's desk. "First leave roster, sir. Do you approve it?"

Grayder sighed wearily. "Mr. Morgan, the basic rule is that everyone on leave must at all times comport himself in a spacemanlike manner, observe and respect all local customs and conventions and do nothing to earn the antagonism of the inhabitants."

"Yes, sir," agreed Morgan. "I'll give them a stiff warning about getting drunk and rowdy."

"I am not bothered about their sobriety or lack of it, Mr. Morgan. I am thinking about their attire."

"Sergeant Major Bidworthy and I invariably check the men for smartness as they go out," Morgan assured. "Any man who has not made himself a credit to the ship is promptly——"

"There are different ideas of what constitutes credit," said Grayder. "Physique, for instance."

"Yes, sir," said Morgan, not seeing what the other was getting at.

Grayder put it bluntly. "Mr. Morgan, I am afraid that the men will have to go out unclothed."

"Without clothes?" An expression of inutterable horror bloomed into Morgan's features. "Naked?"

"That's how it is, Mr. Morgan. These Hygeians are determined faddists. They think it healthier and more decent to go around in the raw. We are not yet in a position to impose better ideas upon them. Therefore we must accept their customs and adapt our own behaviour accordingly. Any men who wish to go to town must do so unclothed."

"But, sir——"

"I am not forbidding leave," Grayder emphasized. "I am conceding the men's right to take time off in a non-hostile world. But I cannot allow a riot to start over the question of somebody's pants. The men must take their liberty in their birthday suits and that's an order."

"Good God!" said Morgan, gulping.

"They can wear boots," put in the Ambassador. "The Hygeians were using sandals."

Shelton, who had rapidly grown crimson in the face, now rasped at Grayder, "What you do with your crew is wholly your own business but I cannot permit my troops to exhibit themselves in nothing but boots."

Not wanting to let Morgan witness an unpleasant clash of

authority, Grayder gave a shrug of resignation, glanced appealingly at the Ambassador.

That person immediately responded by saying, "My dear Colonel, we cannot grant shore-leave to the crew and refuse it to the troops. Privileges must be distributed without fear or favor. To differentiate between the personnel on this ship would be most reprehensible. It could create jealousy, resentment and destroy the cordial relations that exist between the Captain's men and yours."

"I am not denying leave to my men," insisted Shelton. "I am saying that they must go out in ceremonial uniform as prescribed by regulations."

"There are other regulations, Colonel. Captain Grayder has just said it's a strict rule that they must respect local customs. What have you to say to that?"

"It's an equally strict rule that they go out properly dressed."

"The proper dress here is a snazzy pair of sandals," said the Ambassador. "Short of those, we'll have to use boots. Do you accept the full blame for any trouble caused by your men's gross indecency?"

"Heaven!" Shelton burst out. "It is the Hygeians who are indecent."

"Their opinion is the opposite. It is *their* town that the men propose to visit."

Perceiving that this argument could continue forever while the astounded Morgan listened pop-eyed, Grayder interrupted with, "Your Excellency, perhaps the Colonel would be good enough to accept your official order that his men go out undressed."

"Would you?" asked the Ambassador.

"Under strong protest," said Shelton, secretly glad to be rid of the responsibility.

"Very well." The Ambassador spoke to Morgan. "The roster is approved providing that the leave-takers go naked."

Picking up the list, Morgan said feebly, "I don't know what the men will say about this."

"Neither do I," remarked the Ambassador. "But their reactions should be interesting."

Morgan departed, slightly dazed.

5

Ambling morbidly toward the tail-end, Morgan met Gleed and said, "I've got news for you."

"Go ahead," invited Gleed. "Intrigue me."

"You're to get stripped."

"Eh?"

"If you go to town you do it in your pelt."

"Hah, funny," said Gleed.

"It's an order,'" Morgan asserted.

"Whose?—Grayder's? I don't take orders from him."

"It's a joint one issued by His Excellency, the Colonel and the Captain. I'm not kidding you, either. All men who visit that town must do so wearing only their boots and some hair-lotion. You'd better go and prepare your buddies for the shock—I'll tell the crew."

He mooched away, sour-faced. Gleed had a moment of doubt, decided that Morgan was too self-important to descend to childish tricks. He hastened toward the troops' quarters, encountered Bidworthy at the halfway mark.

"Pardon, Sergeant Major," he began with great respect, "do you know anything about this order that men on leave must go out unclothed?"

Bidworthy looked him over very slowly from head to feet and with equal slowness from feet to head. "How much service have you put in?"

"Twenty years."

Nodding profoundly, Bidworthy went on, "Twenty years' service. Three stripes. A full-blown sergeant. And still you listen to barrackroom gab."

"First Mate Morgan told me about it," Gleed protested.

"Then he must have a warped sense of humor," said Bidworthy. "But at your age and with your rank you should know better than to fall for it."

With low cunning, Gleed prompted, "Then it's *your* order that we go in ceremonial uniform?"

"It is not my order at all," denied Bidworthy. "It doesn't

have to be. It's a rigid regulation of which everyone is well aware. What's more, I shall hold the usual inspection to ensure that it is obeyed. There will be trouble for the man I find sloppily dressed." He paused, added with menace, "Even if he happens to be a sergeant."

Before Gleed could think up an adequate reply a trooper stuck his head out of a nearby doorway and said, "Excuse me, Sergeant Major, the Colonel is calling for you on the intercom. Want to answer from here?"

"Yes."

Bidworthy hurried into the room leaving the door wide open. It was too great a temptation for Gleed who remained in the corridor and stretched his ears.

"Sir!" sounded Bidworthy's gruff tones. "Yes, sir. The first roster. *What?*" This was followed by a peculiar choking noise. "Do I hear you aright, sir? You mean actually *nude?* But, sir, the regulations——" More gargling. "I understand, sir. It's an order."

Came the click of a phone being cradled. A period of heavy breathing. When Bidworthy emerged he looked like a sleepwalker. His face somewhat apoplectic, he walked right past Gleed without seeing him.

A minute later Gleed charged into the first dormitory and looked it over with an authoritative eye. A few troopers were lying on their bunks absorbed in books. Several were playing cards. Others were brushing jackets and pressing pants. On the nearest bunk Trooper Piatelli was assiduously shining his heavy boots.

"You on the first roster?" inquired Gleed.

"Yes, Sergeant."

"Then you'd better give those a polish like you've never given them before. Not just a good polish. Not even an excellent polish. Make it a superb polish."

Piatelli asked, "Why?"

"Because," informed Gleed, "those clompers are all you'll be wearing."

"All?" said Piatelli, mystified.

"All is what I said."

"You mean I've been taken off the roster? They've stopped my leave? I can't go out? Why'd they pick on me? I've done nothing wrong."

By now the readers had dropped their books, the players put down their cards, the pants-pressers ceased work. Everyone was staring at Piatelli. Self-consciously he gave the boots a couple of rubs before repeating his complaint.

"Why'd they pick on me?"

"Much as I hate to deprive you of your martyrdom," said Gleed, "I have to state that everyone is picked on. Every mother's son of us. The order is that leave must be taken in the bare, front and back."

"No!" exclaimed the readers.

"No!" chorused the card-players.

"No!" shouted the pants-pressers.

"Yes!" insisted Gleed.

Piatelli flung his boots on the floor. "I'm not taking my leave. I refuse to go."

"Why?" asked Gleed. "Are you adorned with a vulgar tattoo?"

"There'll be lots of women in that town."

"What of it? Your mother was a woman, wasn't she? They can't see any more than she did."

"That's different," said Piatelli.

"If I remember aright," Gleed continued, "you were one of that squad whose physical examination was conducted by a woman. I don't recall you playing hell about it then."

"She was a qualified doctor. Mothers and doctors aren't the same as ordinary women."

"The Hygeian females aren't the same, either. They're a bunch of nakes. What's one more among a million of 'em?"

"I don't care," said Piatelli. "I don't go out without so much as my shorts."

"Cowardice in the face of the enemy," pronounced Gleed. "You surprise me, Piatelli. No spine, no guts."

"That's better than no clothes," Piatelli retorted.

Somebody called impudently, "You're on the first roster, Sarge. Are you going out?"

"Providing I've got company," Gleed said. "There's no fun in fooling around on one's own."

He left the dormitory amid a gabble of voices, went to the next one, gave them the same news. Then to the next and the next. By the time he had finished nobody had yet been informed by Bidworthy, that person having decided that it was bad enough having the accept a breach of regulations without also making himself the instrument of its transmission.

At ten in the morning eight men lined up in the mid airlock. They were decoy ducks for the two hundred others who had decided to postpone going out pending first-hand information on what it was like to stroll around town sans zoot. Five of the eight were former members of sunbathing societies, imperturbable because facing a familiar prospect. One was a physical culture practiner only too willing to exhibit his beautiful body. One was doing it for a bet. The eighth was Gleed, determined to assert every man's right to shore-leave come what may.

Bidworthy arrived, his face flushed in manner suggesting a few preliminary nips at a bottle. Standing squarely before the first man, he shot a swift look of revulsion over the body, concentrated attention upon the boots. It was obvious that he was gravely handicapped by lack of helmets to be adjusted, belts to be tightened, buttons to be fastened. His attitude was the same right along the line until he came to Gleed. There at last he found something to criticize.

"How is it," he inquired with exaggerated politeness, "that I have not been informed of your precipitate demotion?"

Gleed eyed him blankly.

"Where are your stripes?" bawled Bidworthy.

"On my uniform, Sergeant Major," replied Gleed as soothingly as possible. "I am not wearing my uniform right now."

"Is that so? I am indebted to you for the information. I wouldn't have been aware of it if you hadn't drawn my attention to it." He fumed a bit, then roared, "Get those stripes on somehow, I don't care how. Paint them on if necessary. The fact that you're stark doesn't mean you've been discharged from the space service and have ceased to be an N.C.O." With that he marched irefully out, pausing only to look back and say, "God help us!"

"Something seems to be eating Ruthless Rufus," remarked the physical culture expert, expanding his chest and strutting around. "You coming with us, Sarge, or going on your own?"

"I'll have to put these stripes on first. How am I going to do it?"

"Go see Trooper O'Keefe in the fourth dorm," suggested one of the others. "He's got plenty of lipstick."

"All right. Wait for me, you fellows." Gleed went to the fourth dormitory, found O'Keefe sitting on his bunk practising a conjuring trick with two colored balls and a silk handkerchief. The other occupants goggled at the nude arrival with complete lack of respect for rank. Ignoring this, Gleed asked, "Is it a fact that you have some lipstick?"

"Lipstick?" O'Keefe registered great pain. "What d'you think I am?" Extracting a box from under his bunk, he opened it, revealed a jumble of fake playing-cards, wire puzzles and similar stuff. From this mess he dug out a flat tray full of what appeared to be colored candles. "Theatrical greasepaint," he informed. He fished up a false beard, jet black and fluffy. "Want to disguise yourself?"

"No—I've got to show my stripes. I thought maybe you could mark them on my arm."

"Sorry," said O'Keefe, enjoying himself, "but as a common trooper I lack the authority to make you a sergeant."

"Get busy and give me three stripes," threatened Gleed, "or when I come back on duty I'll make everyone's heart bleed for you."

He offered an arm with the muscles bunched. O'Keefe did as ordered. Gleed examined the result, was satisfied. He glanced at the smirking onlookers.

"Well, what are you monkeys chittering at? Never seen a man in the altogether before?"

"It isn't that, Sarge," replied one. "It's the boots. They're incongruous."

"Hah," said Gleed without humor. "We've no sandals and that's that. It's got to be boots." He left them, reached the airlock. "I am now a model of sartorial perfection. Let's go, fellows."

The eight went down the gangway, headed for the faint path the Hygeians had made through the grain, took no notice of personal and pointed comments yelled from the ship. They made good pace, got out of the crops and onto a narrow road leading to the town. There was no traffic upon this road except for what looked like a horse and cart vaguely visible a long way back.

Trooper Yarrow, one of the erstwhile sunbathers, enthused, "Man, this gives me zip! Anything to get away from Bidworthy and that metal bottle for a while. I'd do it on ten-foot stilts if I had to. Don't understand why all the others are so windy."

His boon companion, Trooper Kinvig, said, "Notice something? All troopers. No crew. Not one."

"Yellow-bellies," opined Yarrow.

"Yah, pinkies!" screamed a shrill voice.

They looked mutually toward the source. Two boys of nine, naked and deep brown with sunburn, were sitting atop a wall pointing at them.

"Pinkies!" shrieked one.

"Corpse-bodies!" competed the other, laughing himself silly.

"Take no notice," ordered Gleed, marching on with bare dignity.

"Pinkies!" howled the two in unison. "Sickly dead-flesh!"

"They don't seem to like our complexions," complained Kinvig, unhappy about it.

"We'll be as brown as they are within a few days," Gleed pointed out. "I'm browning as I walk."

"That may be—but I still don't like being compared with a corpse. Who do those kids think they are?"

Now the town hove into near view. So also did two men walking towards them. These oncomers attracted instant attention because both were about seven feet tall and built like prize bulls. They weighed about three hundred pounds apiece. Each was adorned with an inscribed silver disc hanging from his neck by a thin chain.

Stepping into the visitors' path and bringing them to a halt, they surveyed the group with mingled disgust and disdain. One spoke, his voice deep and authoritative.

"You're Terrans?"

"That's obvious, Lashman," observed the second of the pair. "Pale, thin, underweight and ruining their soles with clumsy footgear."

"I know, Fant," said Lashman. "But we have to be formal about this." He returned attention to Gleed, picking on him because of his greasepaint stripes. "Terrans?"

"Yes," said Gleed, accepting the role of spokesman.

"Where are you going?"

"What's it to do with you?" asked Gleed toughly.

"Everything." Lashman pointed to the disc shining on his huge chest. "We are Public Guardians. We are entitled to ask questions. Where are you going?"

"Into town."

"Who gave you permission to do so?"

Not liking the situation nor the enormous size of his opponents, Gleed decided that a little tact would not come amiss. "Our commanding officer. He's had an interview with your Mayor and has since allowed us to go out."

"Then let's see your certificates of fumigation."

"Certificates of *what?*" exclaimed Gleed, thunderstruck.

"Fumigation," repeated Lashman and added in an aside to Fant, "Defective hearing. In need of aural irrigation."

"Canals blocked with dirt," agreed Fant.

At that point the physical culture expert stepped to the front, swelled his muscles and demanded aggressively, "Who says we should be fumigated?"

Reaching out a hand the size of a spade, Lashman picked him up by the scruff of his neck, held him in mid-air and said clearly and distinctly, "Shut up!" Then he put him down. The victim shuffled sheepishly to the back of the bunch. Lashman spoke to Gleed.

"Have you or have you not been fumigated?"

"We're quite clean. We wouldn't have been permitted to leave the ship if we'd been unclean."

"Have you or have you not been fumigated?"

"No, we haven't."

"You can't enter the town unless medically examined and disinfected."

"Yah, waxies!" came a thin cry from the distance.

"Why not?" asked Gleed, disappointed and peeved. "Do you think we're full of disease?"

"The law is the law. If you don't like it, get it altered."

"This is no way to treat friends," Gleed persisted. "If your mayor had objected to us looking around he'd have said so."

"Was he asked?" put in Fant.

"I don't know."

"Then you can take it that he wasn't. What makes you think you can go where you like and do as you please on somebody else's world?"

"I—"

Lashman interrupted. "And why have you left off your coverings? Why are you exposing your revolting bodies for all to see? Don't you know that it is indecent and disgusting?"

"Holy smoke!" Gleed went pop-eyed. "We've been ordered to do as you people do."

"As we do?" Lashman frowned his disapproval. "We don't display bodies anything like yours. If I were one half as feeble and decrepit I'd hang myself from the nearest tree, wouldn't you, Fant?"

"Yaz," said Fant with pious fervor.

"*We* exhibit strong, healthy bodies," insisted Lashman. "Like this one." He slapped his broad abdomen. It sounded like smacking a slab of granite. "Something worth seeing."

"Think you're good, don't you?" interjected Trooper Yarrow with maximum sarcasm.

Lashman stared at him forbiddingly. "Did anyone request you to speak, Skinny-ribs?"

"Let's go back to the ship," said Gleed. "I'll make a report to the Colonel. Maybe he'll take some action about it."

"But what about our leave?" complained Kinvig. "We're being bilked of it."

"What alternative do you suggest?" Gleed invited.

Kinvig couldn't think of any. Neither could the others. A united attack upon the tremendous Public Guardians might be successful but obviously would not gain them the keys to paradise. On the contrary, assault and battery would earn them a court-martial, if they survived to face it.

"I'm returning anyway," Gleed told them. "You crummy-looking nakes can please yourselves."

With that he about-turned and marched off. As expected, the rest followed like sheep while Lashman and Fant gazed contemptuously at the new view.

The group trudged in dismal silence, full of moody thoughts and some ill temper. Presently they came abreast of the wall. A sod of earth arced over it and struck the physical culturist upon his curvature.

"Yow-ha!" sounded a yell of triumph. "Skeletons!"

"Right on target," remarked Gleed with appreciation.

Halting in his tracks, his face inflamed, the stricken one told all and sundry, "I am about to commit murder."

"No you don't," commanded Gleed, grabbing his arm. "Baby-killing isn't in the contract. Keep going, back to the ship. Home sweet home."

"Home," growled Kinvig. "You slay me with your wit."

They paraded onward while shouts of victory and screams of abuse faded away behind. Soon they met the cart previously noticed. It was drawn by a real Earth-horse that rolled its eyes as if it too considered them as an extraordinary spectacle.

Though not as huge as Lashman and Fant, the driver was a powerful, heavily muscled specimen who treated the Terrans to a loud sniff, jiggled his reins and urged the horse from a plod to a slow trot. On top of the cart two teen age girls were sitting three-quarters buried in the load of hay.

Glancing upward as they passed, Trooper Yarrow stopped as if held by an invisible hand, said in tones of delighted reverence, "Look, fellows, real live dames!"

The girls pointed at Yarrow and giggled helplessly. One gasped a remark to the other and that set them off on another burst of merriment. With tears running down their faces, they clung together and boosted themselves to the verge of hysterics as the cart receded.

Yarrow angrily demanded of nobody in particular, "What's supposed to be funny?"

"Us," Gleed told him.

Leaving the road, they took their former route through the fields, arrived at the ship and mounted the gangway one by one. Each had the air of a pilgrim denied salvation for no known sin. In the airlock Tenth Engineer Harrison welcomed them with frank surprise.

"What, so soon?"

"Their frenzied welcome laid us out," Yarrow told him. "We've come back to recuperate."

"Why don't you go and get a taste of it yourself?" inquired Kinvig.

"I intend to. I'm on the third roster."

"What a picture you'll make," said Kinvig maliciously. "Nude on a bike."

He hurried after the others into the ship. Gleed went through the airlock last, looking sour.

"Something wrong?" prompted Harrison.

"Sure is. We stink with our clothes on and we still stink with them off. I'm going to see the Colonel about it."

So saying, he made for the chartroom, knocked, waited a moment and entered. Nobody was there. With a brief under-breath cuss he made his way to the control-room. That was empty too. Finally he traced his quarry to the officers' lounge, knocked again.

A voice responded, "Come in!"

Gleed marched in with military precision. Disregarding a dozen pairs of startled eyes, he halted before Shelton, stood stiffly with head erect and hands pressed grimly against thighs.

"Your pardon, Colonel. I beg to report that——"

Spilling the drink he was holding, Shelton barked, "What the very devil do you mean by appearing before me in *that* disgraceful condition? Completely naked! Good God! Have you gone out of your mind?"

"With all respect, Colonel, men on leave have been ordered to——"

"You are not on leave when in my presence," contradicted Shelton with visible ire. "You are on parade. If a sergeant does not know the regulations what can one expect of the men?"

"Yes, sir, but——"

"Don't you dare pose there without even a lioncloth and argue with me." Shelton spilled more of his drink. "Go and get dressed. I am repelled by the sight of your anatomy. If you wish to see me you must do so in the proper manner."

"Yes, sir," said Gleed, swallowing hard.

He snapped an accurate salute, about-turned and marched out. As he closed the door he heard Shelton say to the others, "Disgraceful! The space service is going to the dogs!"

Arriving at the N.C.O.'s domitory, Gleed kicked off his boots, pulled on his shorts, sat on his bunk and glowered at the metal wall.

"What a life!" he complained. "What a ship! What a world!"

As the news travelled around the ship the men reacted in different ways. A belligerent minority was in favor of going to town, clothed and armed with rubber truncheons, and pounding a few Hygeian heads. The rest philosophically accepted the fact that Terrans were unwanted oddities and swiftly built up a habit of referring to each other as freaks.

This reached its climax when a trooper innocently replied to a question from Bidworthy by saying, "Freak Moran has just gone to the washroom."

"Eh? Who?"

"I mean *Trooper* Moran—Freak Major."

By early afternoon men off duty had found a temporary compromise by leaving the ship but not approaching the town. Some went for walks in the opposite direction, towards the distant forest. A few played handball. The majority were content to repose full length on the soft, cushiony sward, absorbing sunshine and fresh air and idly speculating about what their leaders might do to bring the natives to their senses. Most were of the opinion that no effective action would be or could be taken.

"Space," remarked Trooper Yarrow profoundly, flat on his back and chewing a straw, "is a place where anything can happen—even nothing."

"You said it, freak," supported Kinvig. "Notice how the top brass has carefully refrained from setting an example for low-lifes like us? Does Shelton try to get into town in his skin? Does His Freakiness the Ambassador? They do not! They sit on their butts in the officers' lounge guzzling their drinks and waiting for time to roll past."

"They're afraid to be seen in the raw," opined Trooper Jacobi. "Ninety-nine percent of their authority is located in their uniforms, badges and insignia. I reckon there's a lot to be said in favor of universal nudity. Strip a fellow of his clothes and what have you got? Just another dumb bum."

"Yes, sir," approved Yarrow. "We were born naked. It wouldn't kill us to stay that way."

"It'd save lots of time, trouble and expense," Kinvig contributed.

"I'd give plenty to see Bidworty trying to throw his weight around in nothing but boots," offered Jacobi dreamily.

"I'd give more to watch the Ambassador acting high and mighty a yard behind his own pot belly," Yarrow responded. "I reckon he'd bear close resemblance to a sow in litter."

Trooper Veitch, lying nearby, rolled over, yawned widely and said, "Do I hear subversive propaganda?"

"Quiet, freak," ordered Yarrow.

Gleed appeared, still in shorts and boots, looked down at them. "Been watching the area through powerful glasses for over an hour. It looks as if these Hygeians have no automobiles, no planes, maybe because they've no oil resources either. They have steam locomotives and horses. All their transport seems to be based on locos and horses." He meditated as if he had something special in mind, asked, "Any of you fellows know how to handle a horse?"

"I do," said Veitch, sitting up.

"Good!" approved Gleed. "Sergeant Schneed is a real old nag. Go and report to him for kitchen duty."

Veitch clambered to his feet and displayed much bitterness. "After I get my release I'm going to buy myself a hatchet. Then I'm going to travel around in search of certain people."

"Do I hear subversive propaganda?" inquired Yarrow.

Giving him an ugly look, Veitch ambled toward the gangway. Gleed lay down in his vacated place, gazed at the blue sky and let go a long-drawn sigh of pleasure.

"I'm surprised at Veitch. Seven years' service and still a sucker." The others didn't answer, so he prompted, "Enjoying yourselves, fellows?"

Jacobi said unwarily, "I can think of better things to do."

"How right you are," approved Gleed. "You chase after Veitch and report for kitchen duty."

Very ungraciously, Jacobi departed. Yarrow and Kinvig then decided it might be more comfortable a couple of hundred yards away. They moved before further conversation could bring forth the fact that the kitchen could make good use of them also.

Grinning to himself, Gleed reposed full length and surveyed the sky until his eyes grew heavy. Presently he closed them and drifted into sleep. He had been snoring steadily for an hour when Yarrow nudged him wide awake.

"Sarge, that deputation is coming through the grain again."

Getting up, Gleed had a look, recognized the Mayor and his councillors. He hurried into the airlock, used the phone. Grayder answered.

"Captain, that official party is returning."

"Bring them to the chartroom as before, Sergeant."

"Right, sir."

With his wiskers flapping in the slight breeze, the Mayor mounted the gangway. He was still clinging to his civic totem-pole. The councillors followed except for Gerpongo who remained on the grass, hugged the bag containing his spray-gun and looked at the lolling troops as if he considered them long overdue for treatment.

Gleed led his party to the chartroom door, opened it for them but was careful to keep out of sight himself. For the time being, he felt, it would be wise to avoid the irate Shelton's gaze. What the eye does not see the brasshat mind cannot bellow over.

The Mayor and his councillors filed in, grouped themselves as before. Stroking his beard and raising his totem-pole, the Mayor addressed His Excellency.

"Health be yours."

"Thank you," said the Ambassador, thinking this health business could be taken a bit too far.

"We have consulted our government and after due consideration they have decided to agree with your suggestions," enunciated the Mayor.

"Ah!" exclaimed the Ambassador delightedly.

"Upon certain conditions."

The delight vanished as swiftly as it had come. "What conditions?"

Producing a map from his shoulder-bag, the Mayor unfolded it, put it on Grayder's desk and planted a wrinkled finger upon it. "You will see that at this point, which is not far north of here, the great river Sambar splits and flows on either side of an island. It is a very nice island, verdant and healthy. It covers almost a thousand acres and is ideal for an isolation camp."

"Isolation?" echoed the Ambassador, frowning.

"You can take over that island on the understanding that your men remain there for a quarantine period of one year."

"Quarantine?"

"They may not leave the island and mix among our people before this one year is through. And then they must submit to medical examination and disinfection by us. Any men not considered healthy enough to let loose must stay on the island until such time as we find them physically fit in all respects. With regard to these matters our decisions shall be accepted as final."

"Is that all?" asked the Ambassador.

"Indeed, no. It is understood that you will place upon this island your consul, his staff and bodyguard, also two long-range transmitters with their appropriate technicians. Having done so, you will not at later date increase their numbers without first obtaining our consent."

"Anything more?"

"Yaz," said the Mayor, wetting his lips. "If after one year a number of Terrans are permitted to travel where they please they will not disgust the populace by wearing clothes. We cannot allow the minds of our children to be perverted by such filthy exhibitionism. Terrans must justify their freedom by behaving with common decency, as we do. That is not too much to ask."

"I suppose not," admitted the Ambassador, slightly whirly.

"Lastly," finished the Mayor, "if in due time romantic associations should arise and it should be considered expedient to solemnize marriages between these Terrans and our people, such marriages will be recognized by you as legal and valid. By that is meant that the bridegroom will be entitled to permanent residence upon Hygeia. You will not have the right to compel him to desert his wife and family by transferring him to another world."

Shelton interrupted with, "There's a nice way for a malcontent to opt out of the space service whenever he feels like it."

"He could scoot in any case," the Ambassador pointed out. "All he need do is throw his clothes in the river and join the naked herd."

"Not legally," said Shelton.

"If half the consular bodyguard takes to the woods what does it matter whether their action is legal or illegal," asked the Ambassador. "They've vanished just the same."

"We don't have to encourage it by providing a legal loophole," Shelton protested.

Before the Ambassador could frame a suitable reply the Mayor spoke severely. "You are taking a lot for granted— and without any visible justification."

"What d'you mean?" asked Shelton.

"You appear to be under the delusion that all your men are irresistible charmers and that our women will consider it a great privilege to marry them."

"What's wrong with marrying a Terran trooper?"

Now the Ambassador interrupted. "My dear Colonel let us keep to the subject, for heaven's sake. We have something better to do than discuss the merits of Terran-Hygeian wedded bliss. What we have to consider are the terms on which representation may be established upon this planet." Then he turned to the Mayor. "Excuse me—I won't be a minute."

He went out, hurried to the lounge, found Lieutenant Deacon there. "Lieutenant, I'd like you to conduct the mayoral party here while we talk over their proposals in private. Seat them comfortably and provide them with drinks." He favored the other with a fat wink. "Plenty of drinks."

"Plenty?" repeated Deacon.

"That's what I said. These nudists are far too healthy, smug and self-satisfied for my liking. I think it might be a good thing if the Mayor had to be carried home blowing fumes through his whiskers. I hope you grasp my meaning, Lieutenant."

"Yes, Your Excellency—I'll tend to it."

Returning followed by Deacon, the Ambassador said to the Hygeians, "We'd like to discuss your conditions between ourselves, if you don't mind. The Lieutenant will take you to the lounge. We'll inform you of our decision as soon as possible."

Raising no objection, the Mayor and his men departed in the wake of Deacon. When they had gone, the Ambassador rubbed his hands together and spoke briskly.

"Let's not get side-tracked. There's only one question to answer—do we accept their proposition or do we not?"

"I don't like it," said Shelton moodily.

"Your reasons?"

"They're dictating terms to us instead of us to them."

"It's their world," offered Grayder.

"It'll be *our* grief if they're attacked from outside," Shelton retorted. "Since our strength is considerable while theirs is negligible the brunt of the battle will fall upon us. If they want Terran protection they should buy it at our price."

"You think there's a seller's market in protection, eh?" asked the Ambassador.

"Sure there is. We have the arms, ships and men. We have the industrial power, the productive capacity, the technical know-how. The Hygeians have nothing worth mentioning, not even clothes."

"That may be so," the Ambassador said. "But where's the seller's market without a buyer?"

"They're buying all right—otherwise they wouldn't have decided to accept our offer."

"I'm not so sure about that. I don't think they really consider themselves in danger of alien invasion or that they really want a mutual defence pact. I suspect that they're playing ball, within limits, in the hope of getting something out of it. It wouldn't surprise me if they didn't try to turn our own story against us; they'll use this hypothetical threat as an excuse to cadge machine-tools from us. Or anything else they need." The Ambassador looked at Grayder. "What are your views?"

"Half a loaf is better than no bread."

"I agree. This island they've offered us will be a Terran foothold even if a small, restricted one. At later date some pretext will be found for expanding it. After all, the authorities can't expect us to zoom around confiscating entire planets with the limited force on this one ship. If high policy requires that we get tough let them send out the fleet." He thought awhile, finished, "If we accept the Hygeian offer we'll have achieved what we were sent out to do. I'm in favor of accepting and leaving our powers-that-be to cope with any subsequent quibbles. What do you say?"

"We've two more planets yet to visit," reminded Grayder. "Nobody knows what complications we'll have to face on those. Or how much time it will take. The sooner we finish with this one and move on, the better."

"I can't outvote the two of you," said Shelton with bad grace.

"That makes it unanimous," declared the Ambassador. "Let us go tell them and join their drunken celebration."

6

The Mayor greeted them with, "You have strange ideas of hospitality." He pointed his pole at Deacon. "He invited us to ruin our digestive tracts with alcohol."

"It's a Terran custom," explained the Ambassador, taken aback.

"I don't doubt that," responded the Mayor, accepting that Terrans were capable of any iniquity. "If it pleases you to degenerate into hopeless sots, that is wholly your own affair. But don't expect us to join you in such depravity. There is only one drink fit for a healthy mind in a healthy body." He turned to his councillors. "And what is that?"

"Pure, clear water," they chorused.

"You should examine water through a powerful microscope," the Ambassador suggested. "It looks like germ-soup."

"Probably it does—on Terra," agreed the Mayor. "And if this ship's tanks are full of the stuff you're welcome to it." He dismissed the unpleasant subject with a gesture, went on,

'Have you reached a decision? What do you want me to tell our government?"

"We accept their offer."

"And how soon will you be ready to disembark the men and equipment?"

"We'll have to transfer the ship to the island or somewhere adjacent providing there's a suitable landing-place in that locality. We can't dump it anywhere because we can sit only on solid bedrock."

"The island won't do. It has woods, gardens and cultivated fields. Also a number of buildings including an excellent gymnasium. That's what your men could really do with, a gymnasium, isn't it?"

"Maybe."

"Landing a vessel this size would create a lot of unnecessary destruction," the Mayor asserted. "As for the areas on either side of the Sambar, they are soft earth and full of farms. I think it would be easiest to discharge your men and supplies right here."

"And how will they get to the island?" inquired the Ambassador.

"We'll provide horse transport for all the heavy stuff. The men themselves can walk."

"Walk?" echoed the Ambassador.

"Walk?" exclaimed Shelton as if he'd never heard of such a thing.

"A three days' march won't kill them," the Mayor said. "They can't be all that feeble."

The Ambassador appealed to Grayder. "Couldn't we use one or two of the ship's lifeboats?"

"No, Your Excellency."

"Why not?"

"They aren't designed for short hops."

"This is a nice fix. We bring men thousands of millions of miles in the very latest type of superfast spaceship and then expect them to go the rest of the way on their feet."

"What are feet for?" asked the Mayor.

Unable to concoct a telling reply to that question, the Ambassador evaded it by saying, "All right. We'll unload our men and supplies here."

"Can you have them ready early tomorrow morning?"

"I suppose so. Why?"

"We'll cut a track through the fields and have a horse-and-cart convoy up the hill by that time. It would be best to start the journey as soon as possible so that the travellers will have a full day ahead of them. Chronic drinkers and smokers will totter along at only half our pace."

"You don't know my space-troopers," interjected Shelton with some annoyance.

"Let it pass, Colonel," ordered the Ambassador. Then to the Mayor, "We'll be ready in the morning."

"Then I'll inform the government and make the necessary preparations."

Lieutenant Deacon led the party out. At the bottom of the gangway there was the usual parade while Gerpongo went through his delousing act. For some time the Ambassador stood by an observation-port watching their progress until they emerged from the fields and onto the road.

"I have a feeling," he said, "that those raw boys are eager to be rid of us. The sooner we depart for the next planet the better they'll like it."

"Maybe they're planning to cut every Terran throat the moment we've gone," hazarded Shelton.

"Nonsense, Colonel. They have everything to gain and nothing to lose by keeping their side of the bargain."

"Then why should they want us out of the way?"

"The motive is psychological," said the Ambassador, looking profound. "They don't mind having some of our men around, especially since they can point to them as an inferior species. But they don't like the presence of this ship. It's a symbol of power. They can exhibit nothing to compete with it. They have no ships themselves and they'll be glad to see the last of this one."

"It won't break my heart to part, either," Shelton assured. "I've had enough of nudity and impertinence."

Taking a small book from his pocket the Ambassador consulted it. "I have available three consuls each with a staff of twenty civil servants. Maybe I had better ask whether any one of them would like this post on Hygeia. I don't want to start giving orders unless I have to. A volunteer is better than a conscript."

"My instructions are that the bodyguard must also be chosen on a voluntary basis," informed Shelton disapprovingly.

"What's wrong with that?"

"Regulations demand that a consular bodyguard shall be of not less than company strength: two officers, eight N.C.O.'s and forty men. Where am I if less than that number offer to go?"

"You'll have to cajole them somehow."

"With all respect, Your Excellency, a commanding officer does not cajole his subordinates."

"Well, convince the reluctant ones that the alternative will be prolonged suffering at your hands. You then get more men than you need."

"Bidworthy is the man to handle it," said Shelton. "I'll pass it to him—that's what he's for."

He hustled away in search of that character.

An hour later Bidworthy paraded D Company in the troops' quarters. Standing aggressively before them, he examined them with a jaundiced eye, cleared his throat and gave forth in manner that brooks no argument.

"A body guard is required for the Terran Consul about to be placed on this planet. The following men have volunteered: Abelson, Adams, Allcock, Baker, Barker, Bunting——" In the same tone of voice he ran right through D Company's roster to the last man, then barked, "All you volunteers will parade in full kit outside the midway airlock at eight hours tomorrow. Any absentees will be charged with mutinous conduct and dealt with accordingly."

That done, he sprayed them with a challenging glare. In spite of this, Trooper Yensen took one step forward and spoke nervously.

"Your pardon, Sergeant Major, but I didn't give my name for——"

"What?" shouted Bidworthy. "What d'you mean?" He waved his list in Yensen's face. "It's down here, isn't it?"

"I suppose so, Sergeant Major," Yensen faltered.

"You suppose so? You actually *suppose* so? Do you dare to doubt my word?" Straightening the paper with a jerk, he held it before the other's eyes, pointed with a thick finger. "Whose name is *that?*"

"Mine," admitted Yensen.

"Then it's on the list. You can't volunteer one minute and devolunteer the next."

"But, Sergeant Major——"

"Silence! If you don't know your own mind I'm the man to make it up for you." He added with menace thick enough to hang in the air like smoke, "You wouldn't care for your name to appear on some *other* list, would you?"

"No, Sergeant Major," said Yensen, suddenly leery. He took a pace back into the ranks and brooded.

"Anyone else want to quibble?" asked Bidworthy, ready to summon a firing squad.

Nobody responded.

"Right. Eight hours. Full kit."

He clanked away on steel-shod boots, entered the chartroom, saluted. "I have to report, sir, that D Company volunteered to a man."

"Did they really?" said Shelton, proud and gratified. "That's fine. Thank you, Sergeant Major."

It had to be admitted that within their peculiar limits the Hygeians were fast-moving and efficient. A bunch of them worked in the night and cut a path eight feet wide through the standing grain. Soon after dawn a dozen horses and carts appeared, trundled creakily to the top of the ridge and lined up near the gangway. With them came twelve over-muscled Public Guardians and one sharp-nosed, shrewd-eyed character who wore a pair of ornamental garters above his knees. This last person had himself taken to the chartroom where he gave forth with official formality.

"Health be yours."

"Thank you," said the Ambassador, staring fascinatedly at the garters.

"I am Smaile of the Ministry." Digging some papers out of his shoulder-bag, he put them on the desk. "I have brought two documentary copies of the agreement negotiated by Mayor Bouchaine. We have signed and now require your signature also."

"Right." The Ambassador felt for his pen.

"I have been told to draw to your attention an extra clause that we have decided to include," Smaile added. Picking up a copy, he read it aloud. "The Terran Consul upon this planet shall be regarded as his world's representative to the whole of Hygeia and not to any specific part thereof."

"What does that mean?" asked the Ambassador suspiciously.

"If the Douks want to dicker with you Terrans they must do so through us. You may not appoint another representative specifically for them. They have no government anyway. They don't recognize anyone's authority except insofar as it suits them to do so. Ours is the only established government upon Hygeia. You must deal with us and with nobody else."

After some thought, the Ambassador said, "I see nothing wrong with that. There's no point in us taking up with a small, unorganized group of pious anarchists."

He signed the agreement with a flourish, handed back one copy. Smaile carefully put it in his bag, spoke again.

"Do your men intend to travel clothed or unclothed?"

"Why?"

"The shortest route to their destination lies through two

towns and eight large villages. If your men insist upon keeping themselves covered they'll have to by-pass those places and add fifteen to twenty miles to their journey. We cannot permit a parade of blatant immorality through our centers of population."

"Some people will see them no matter which way they go," the Ambassador pointed out.

"Yaz, unfortunately," admitted Smaile. "And they will be offended by a procession of the filthy-minded. Can't you persuade them to undress and at least look decent?"

"No, I can't. The Consul has flatly refused to accept his post if he has to go to it naked. I talked him into it only by promising that he can wear what he pleases. The same applies to the whole of his staff."

"If their idea of high diplomacy is to advertise their lewdness for all to see," opined Smaile, "they won't make much progress on this world. But I suppose that even the most depraved of Terrans is not beyond reform. Given enough time we may cure them—I hope."

"There's room for it," conceded the Ambassador, thinking of the chosen Consul who was a tall, weedy sample with a red-tipped nose and a perpetual snuffle. He waited until Smaile had departed, then said to the others, "They seem touchy about these Doukhobors in spite of the fact that they're few in numbers. It's evident that they regard them as as unmitigated nuisance. I must emphasize this in may report to Terra. A time may come when we'll find it very convenient to rush to the rescue of an oppressed minority."

"Think we should try to make contact with the Douks while we're here?" Shelton suggested.

"The idea is tempting but I don't think it wise. It might spoil the present set-up. We'll save them until we need them as an excuse for something or other."

"Such as?" prompted Grayder.

"Well, if at later date Terra finds it expedient to become rough with these Hygeians we can use the Douks as some sort of justification. At immense cost and great sacrifice we shall be liberating them from cruel masters. You must remember, my dear Captain, that whatever Terra sees fit to do is invariably done from the loftiest of motives. There is nothing materialistic or sordid about our space policy. It is born of far-sighted wisdom, high ideals and spiritual values. Isn't that so, Colonel?"

"Yaz," said Shelton absentmindedly.

"A linguist," commented the Ambassador. "Three days and he speaks the local language with complete fluency."

"Eh? What's that, Your Excellency?" asked Shelton, waking up.

"Forget it. Let us go and witness our first memorable step towards claiming an empire."

He left the room, the others following. They reached the airlock, stood at the top of the gangway and looked down.

Already the carts were loaded. The first four bore the parts of two long-range transmitters. The fifth held the smaller and lighter receivers. All the components of a big antenna were in the sixth. A small atomic engine and a large generator occupied the seventh and eighth. The remaining four were piled high with personal luggage plus a generous stock of health-ruining alcohol and tobacco.

Near the bottom of the gangway a disillusioned-looking civil servant was chain-smoking with more speed than enthusiasm. Nearby two Public Guardians and one cart driver showed unconcealed revulsion. The smoker let go a racking cough; the onlookers exchanged a glance of mutual understanding. The smoker coughed again and the others backed away hastily.

Farther out D Company stood in three ranks burdened to the ears with arms and equipment. Not one man showed any sign of giving way to transports of delight. They posed in glum silence, each bent forward with the weight of stuff on his chest and back.

Bidworthy marched slowly along the lines, inspecting them front and rear. It was his last chance to remind this particular bunch that their parents had made a ghastly mistake. He knew it and they knew it. But he was seriously handicapped by two facts: firstly, the top brass was watching and, secondly, there was no way of ordering punishment for an offender soon to depart.

In the middle of the rear rank he came to a dead stop and stared at Trooper Bunting. The object of his attention was blissfully unaware of this scrutiny because nothing was visible save the pair of boots immediately in front of him. As burdened as a Christmas tree, Trooper Bunting was wearing a size ten helmet on a size seven head with the inevitable result that it appeared to rest on his shoulders.

Surveying this apparition with slowly purpling face, Bidworthy let his gaze drift to the next man and there found the opposite effect. Trooper Veitch had a size seven helmet perched like a pimple on top of a size ten cranium. Veitch fidgeted uneasily; he knew that he was about to be picked on but for the life of him could not imagine why.

"Veitch," said Bidworthy in strangled tones.

"Yes, Sergeant Major?"

"Are you compos mentis?"

"How's that again, Sergeant Major?"

"Is that your own helmet?"

"I think somebody squashed it a bit, Sergeant Major," explained Veitch apologetically. "A lot of stuff got tossed around when the ship——"

"Don't give me that!" yelled Bidworthy. He snatched the two helmets, swapped them around, slapped them back on the other's heads. Both fitted. Bunting was vaguely surprised, Veitch astonished. "When they inducted you two dopes," declared Bidworthy in clarion tones, "they were scraping the bottom of the barrel." Snorting like an angry warhorse, he tramped to the front, halted before the officer in command of D Company, saluted and rasped, "All present and correct, sir."

Now the carts started forward and lumbered down the slope with brake-blocks squeaking. The Consul and his staff straggled behind without rhythm or array as is customary with civilians. D Company slung weapons from shoulders, started a precise march made difficult by the slow pace of those ahead of them, a funereal tread more suitable for following a coffin with a flag over it. A torrent of fond farewell's rained upon them from the ship's open ports.

"Where's the body?"

"Hey, Markovitch, you've left your pants on."

"Give 'em hell, boys!"

"Bellies in, chests out—c'mon, smarten up, you bums!"

"Onward Christian soldiers."

"Silence!" roared Bidworthy.

"Ain't nobody here named Silas," informed a voice from the ship.

"Who's that?" Bidworthy yelled, trying to survey two hundred ports at once.

"Who dat say 'Who dat'?" responded the voice mockingly. "Is you where you is or is you ain't?"

Bidworthy made a vengeful dash for the gangway, raced up it, shot through the airlock with a brief, "Pardon me, Colonel," and disappeared into the ship.

"Look out!" warned another voice. "The bull has broken loose!"

Grayder remarked meditatively, "Discipline is the thing."
Shelton said nothing.

When the last of the cavalcade had ambled from sight the
Ambassador said, "That's that!" He returned with the others to
the lounge, poured himself a generous drink, sprawled in a
chair. "We have now a foothold on Hygeia. It is Terra's responsibility to enlarge and strengthen it as time goes on."

"Yes, Your Excellency," said Shelton.

"I'll make out an official report describing what has been
done. Will you have it transmitted as swiftly as possible, Captain?"

"Certainly, Your Excellency," assured Grayder.

"Good!" He sipped his drink, went on, "Now that this job
is finished we might as well push on to the next one. I know
of no irresistible attractions that make it worth our while to
remain here. We have nothing to gain by hanging around.
What do you say?"

"I'll have to see First Mate Morgan before we can go."

"Morgan? Why? What has he got to do with it? He is not
in charge of this ship."

"The men are entitled to liberty. I cannot deprive them of
that right without their consent. Morgan organizes the rosters
and only he can tell me whether the men are willing to go
on or whether they insist on taking their leave in full."

The Ambassador pulled a face. "All right, you consult him.
Tell him we want to depart as soon as possible."

Grayder phoned for Morgan and when he arrived said,
"Mr. Morgan, we plan to boost away just as soon as the men
are ready—what is the position with regard to their liberty?"

"Not so good, sir. The fellows want lots of life, female
company and fun. They aren't getting it. Some refuse to exhibit themselves naked. Those who are willing to undress
have found that they aren't allowed in town. That leaves them
with nothing to do except lie in the grass or mooch around the
fields. I think most of them are pretty fed up."

"They may be luckier next time," Grayder suggested. "It's
hardly likely that yet another planet will view us as vermin."

"No, sir," agreed Morgan, frowning.

"See the men and put it to them," ordered Grayder. "Let me
know as soon as you can whether they are willing to forego
their remaining leave for the sake of getting someplace better."

It was two hours before Morgan returned with the news.
"All the fellows I can find, sir, are in favor of leaving this
world and trying the next one. But a party of ten had left for

walk to the forest and said they wouldn't be back before late in the afternoon."

"Why have they gone there?" asked Grayder. "Just for the troll?"

"That's right, sir. They said they didn't think any big, fat cops would be waiting to heave them out of the woods. Sergeant Gleed's squad is also absent, sir. He marched them away to a nearby farm about an hour ago."

"What for?" put in Shelton suspiciously.

"Tenth Engineer Harrison tells me that Sergeant Gleed got talking to two local nudies named Boogle and Pincuff who were working in the fields this morning. He fed them a story about how we'd lacked a balanced diet since birth and how the Terran authorities kept us in subjection by depriving us of nourishment." Morgan showed the embarrassment of one not sure whether he was being sneaky. "He complimented them repeatedly on their magnificent manhood, made a number of envious remarks about their physique and finally cadged from them two cartloads of fresh vegetables and fruit. He's taken his squad to help load up."

Shelton clapped a hand to his forehead. "A space-trooper panhandling like a hobo. A sergeant behaving like a whining mendicant. A *sergeant* of all people."

"He should be a lieuteannt at least," opined the Ambassador, smacking his lips as thought of fruit and fresh vegetables.

"I'll have him on the carpet for this," swore Shelton. "I'll——"

"No you won't," the Ambassador contradicted. "We cannot share the loot without condoning the crime. And I intend to share the loot."

"But, Your Excellency, discipline——"

"Discipline my fanny," said the Ambassador rudely. "Fruit is really something. I am more than tired of dog-food out of a can. For what we are about to receive may the Lord make us truly thankful." He brightened as another thought struck him and added, "If a sergeant can cadge' two cartloads a colonel should be able to get ten."

"I would not demean myself by telling lies to the natives," declared Shelton.

"Not even for a big, beautiful melon all to yourself?"

"Positively not!"

"Then it's a good thing we've got sergeants," said the Ambassador.

Grayder ended the discussion with, "Mr. Morgan, we'll leave when the last man has returned. Advise me immediately the roll is complete."

"Very well, sir."

By eventide everyone was aboard. So also were the fresh vegetables and fruit. Bidworthy caught the load going through the airlock, goggled as six sacks of rosy apples were lugged past him.

"Sergeant Gleed, where did you procure all this stuff?"

"From that farm over there, Sergeant Major."

"With the farmer's knowledge and consent?"

"Good heavens, Sergeant Major," said Gleed, wounded to the soul, "you don't think we'd rob the place during his absence, do you?"

"I have been in the space service for twenty-five years," informed Bidworthy, "which is plenty long enough to teach me that the only crime is that of being found out." He put on a look of deep cunning. "All right, Gleed how much did you pay this farmer and with what did you pay him?"

"I didn't give him anything."

"You persuaded him to donate two cartloads of fresh food?"

"That's right."

"For nothing?"

"That's right."

"He was fascinated by your personal charm, I suppose?"

"That's right," said Gleed with equanimity.

"You're a liar," stated Bidworthy. "And you know you're a liar. Furthermore, you know that I know you're a liar." He challenged the other with his eyes. "Don't you?"

"Yes, Sergeant Major," said Gleed.

"I am now going to check weapons and stores," announced Bidworthy. "If I find any gaps where you have swapped government material for this dollop of fodder you may expect the balloon to go up. The Colonel will tear off your stripes with his own two hands."

So saying, he dipped fingers into a passing sack, took out a crimson, juicy apple half the size of his head, and clanked away.

An hour later the gangway was drawn in. The airlock closed, the warning siren sounded and the ship lifted. Trooper Casartelli gazed wistfully through an observation-port as the planet shrank beneath.

"Man," he enthused, "that world has most everything: good, solid earth, sunshine, clear air, fruit and flowers. Also several millions of luscious pin-ups wearing nothing but their glorious hair. An Eden crammed with wonderful Eves."

"I didn't see any," said Trooper O'Keefe. "Did you?"

"No, unfortunately. But they're there, man, they're there."

He gave a deep sigh. "Those fellows in D Company were born lucky."

Trooper Yarrow put in with malice, "I didn't notice you falling over yourself in your haste to volunteer."

"Ruthless Rufus didn't give me the chance."

"Ha-ha," said Yarrow sceptically.

"Anyway, if I had offered my name he'd have turned me down dead flat. You know what he's like. He can smell a rat where there isn't one."

"Maybe it's just as well," opined Yarrow. "The Hygeian lovelies will fall only for a healthy mind in a healthy body. You've got neither."

"Speak for yourself, Emaciated," snapped Casartelli.

He remained watching through the port while Hygeia diminished to a tiny half-moon barely discernible alongside a blazing sun. Then he pussyfooted along to Bidworthy's little cabin and swiped that person's apple.

7

The next world had a sun younger and bigger than Sol. It was sixth in a family of eleven planets, had about the same size and mass as Terra. Seven tiny moons circled it closely.

Viewing it in the visiscreen, the Ambassador asked, "Which one is this?"

"Kassim," said Grayder.

"What is known about it?"

"Very little. It was confiscated by three-quarters of a million followers of a crank named Kassim who tried to unite Mohammedanism and Buddhism by claiming to be the reincarnation of the Prophet of Allah. The Moslem world gave them a rough time until they cleared out."

"They were Asiatic religious nuts, so to speak?"

"Yes, Your Excellency."

"Then we know in advance what to expect. They'll insist that we wear slippers and remove them every time we cross a doorstep. They'll demand that we carry prayer-rugs with us wherever we go. Ten times a day they'll want us to prostrate ourselves and salaam to the east. They won't recognize me unless I become teetotal and wash myself only with my left hand."

"I wouldn't be surprised," admitted Grayder.

"That means I shall have to find a consul dopey enough to conform," continued the Ambassador morbidly. "I can choose for myself the world on which I shall take up residence in person. I don't fancy living among a crowd of off-beat Moslems."

"So far as our present trip is concerned, Your Excellency," said Grayder, "you have little choice left. It's either this world or the next one. Four widely spaced planets are as many as we can visit before we return to Terra for a complete overhaul."

"I know. There were only four on the list."

"Well, if none of them pleases you I'm afraid you'll have to wait until our next journey to seek one that does. I don't know when that will be. Neither do I know where we'll be going."

"Your succeeding jaunts are not for me," the Ambassador replied. "My instructions are to establish myself on one world as chief executive over the other three. Terra has a mile long line-up of consuls and ambassadors ready for other ships and other journeys. I'm stuck with this lot. Naturally, I want to select the best of the four. If the next two are even less attractive than the last two——"

"What will you do then?" inquired Grayder interestedly.

"I think I'll transfer the fellow on Hygeia and take over there myself. It would give me a definite pain in the neck but at least I'd have the consolation of knowing that the other places are worse."

"Hygeia is a paradise compared with some places I've heard about," observed Grayder.

"I suppose so. I'll take it for lack of anything better. That is my right. I'm the senior Terran representative. The consuls are comparative juniors. A junior must suffer to qualify as a senior. I don't believe in people gaining promotion the easy way, do you, my dear Captain?"

"Certainly not," said Grayder.

He went to the control-room and took charge. Already cameras were recording the approach. Soon they began taking hemispheric pictures as the ship swung round the sunlit side and back again into the dark. Carefully the great vessel closed in, circling the world at rapidly decreasing altitude.

Land and seas expanded, revealing more and more details. Soon it could be seen that this planet was far more lush than the previous ones. The hot sun burned through thin banks of cloud upon sparkling oceans and shining rivers, cast light and shadow over huge masses of tangled vegetation.

Here and there, mostly alongside or near to rivers, were vaguely discernible clearings marked with what might be roads and buildings; the characteristic markings of humanity at work. But these areas were small and their number was few. The ship went lower while cameras continued to operate. It circled the world another ten times and then went up.

Soon afterward the Ambassador arrived in the control-room. "I've been having a look, Captain. There is an awful lot of jungle."

"Sure is, Your Excellency."

"And not much else. It surprises me. All these years and they've practically nothing to show for them. You said that three-quarters of a million came here, didn't you?"

"That is what's in the ancient records."

"Perhaps the records are unreliable. It doesn't look to me as if their total strength amounts to that many even today. They've hardly scratched the place." He took a glance through the nearest port in spite of the fact that the ship was now far too high for accurate observation. "There is something mighty peculiar about this. It isn't like Asiatics to reduce their numbers so drastically. I expected to find this world exceptionally well populated."

"So did I."

"Oh, well, we'll solve the mystery before long. Have you found a good landing-place, Captain?"

"Not yet, Your Excellency. I am waiting for the enlargements of our closest photographs."

"Yes, of course. You'll have to choose with great care. We cannot afford to spend weeks laboriously hacking our way to the nearest village."

He sat down and frowned thoughtfully until the photos arrived. Grayder spread them on his desk, examined them in silence one by one, passing each in turn to the Ambassador. Finally Grayder put his finger in the middle of a picture.

"Have a look at this, Your Excellency."

The Ambassador stared at the part indicated. "H'm! Quite a large village. Not a good, sharp picture, though. It is badly blurred."

"You haven't the trained eyes for these blown-up jobs taken from directly above." Grayder pointed to a wall cabinet. "Put it in that stereoscopic viewer and have another look."

Doing as instructed, the Ambassador fitted his face into

the rubber eyepiece, gazed at the scene now shown clearly in three dimensions. He let go a hoarse grunt.

"Deserted and overgrown," he reported. "All the buildings are ruins. Don't look as if they've been used for many years. No roads or paths leading anywhere. The jungle has closed in."

"That's one," said Grayder grimly. "All the others are the same." He handed across a bunch of photographs to prove it and after the Ambassador had scanned them, prompted, "Well?"

"It's sheer guesswork but it seems to me this world has been dead for at least a century. I can't see the slightest evidence of present life."

"Neither can I."

"Something must have caused it."

"Something must," agreed Grayder.

The Ambassador displayed sudden alarm. "What we have been fearing may already have happened. They've been attacked without warning and destroyed to the last man."

"I don't think so."

"Why not?"

"Any lifeform capable of extending its wars into cosmic space," said Grayder patiently, "must have a good deal of intelligence even if no morals. Intelligent people don't attack and destroy just for the hell of it. They need a motive. Usually the motive is conquest." He jerked a thumb toward the port. "If unknown aliens have wiped out every human being on that planet they'd now be in possession. And we'd see plenty of evidence of their existence." Then he added dryly, "In fact we'd be darned lucky not to be attacked ourselves."

"I can agree with your first point but not with your last," said the Ambassador. "Their war-fleet could have dumped a small number of colonists and moved on. After all, there are plenty of Terran worlds quite incapable of defending themselves against an unexpected intruder."

"Anything is possible, Your Excellency," allowed Grayder. He pointed to the photographs. "But there is not one sign of alien occupation. Moreover, it is obvious that those villages have been or are being destroyed by time and the jungle, not by warfare."

"Yes, I admit they look that way to me." The Ambassador pondered a minute, came up with another theory. "We don't know the real nature of that jungle. It isn't necessarily dangerous or menacing. On the contrary it may be crammed with food and provide perfect shelter, thus creating an irresistible temptation to revert to the apes. Perhaps they're all living in the jungle right now. Just a gang of happy animals scratching themselves, guzzling bananas and slinging the skins at each other."

"Must have taken them a long, long time to see the easy way," observed Grayder. "They did plently of sweating before it dawned upon them that they need not bother."

"You're arguing on the assumption that religious cranks can be trusted to behave rationally," the Ambassador gave back. "But they don't. If their inspired leader orders them to clear away the jungle and build a hundred heavenly places they'll slave like maniacs to do it. Then if he gets a sudden revelation that salvation lies in everyone becoming Tarzans they'll abandon their handiwork and take to the trees. They'll squat on the branches and gibber in alphabetical order whenever he rings the bell. Ye gods, Captain, if these fellows had been halfway sane they'd never have left Terra in the first place."

"Even so, a mulish minority would have remained in their villages and kept their homes in good repair. New generations usually produce an opposition to the ways of their elders." Again he pointed to the pictures. "I don't like the complete unanimity with which they had disappeared. It looks bad to me."

"I see no point in us circling at a safe distance while we theorize about it," remarked the Ambassador. "There is nothing to stop us going down and discovering the truth for ourselves. If you can find a suitable landing-place, let's use it."

"I daren't," said Grayder.

The other stared at him in surprise. "Why not? What's to prevent us? We have definite orders to land on every planet and make a full report about it."

"That does not apply to any world actually or apparently dead," Grayder informed.

"Who says so?"

"It is a basic rule of space navigation, Your Excellency."

"Is it? That's the first I've heard of it. What is the reason?"

"The deadliest enemies of mankind are contagious diseases, especially alien ones to which we have no natural resistance. If on any planet it is found that Terran colonists have been decimated or exterminated the assumption is that a virulent germ may be responsible."

"So you think that this lot may have been wiped out by an epidemic?"

"I don't know. But I'm taking no chances. I cannot accept

the risk of landing, picking up a consignment of germs and transporting them to the next world or even to Terra. I have no desire to go down in history as a bigger and better version of Typhoid Mary."

"Well, I can't say I blame you, Captain. This rule you've mentioned is a new one on me but I admit that it makes sense. The effect of it is that all ships are forbidden to land on any planet that may be riddled with disease, eh?"

"Yes."

"Which means that even the most desirable one can be banned to humanity for everlasting? And on the strength of a mere suspicion?"

"Oh, it's not as bad as that. Terra is building a special ship for remotely controlled exploration of difficult or dangerous worlds. It will be full of robotic equipment and carry a load of scientific experts. I don't know how soon it will be ready but doubtless it will be able to examine this planet and find out what went wrong."

"Well, that's a comfort," approved the Ambassador. "I don't like the idea of unsolved mysteries floating around in space, especially in the sector for which I am responsible. It's plenty bad enough to become official keeper of a cosmic mortuary; I'd like to know how many cadavers are in my charge and what made them that way."

Shelton came in and asked, "What's delaying us, Captain? Is there something wrong?"

"The place looks dead."

"Probably they've cut each other's throats," hazarded Shelton with indecent gusto. "Oddities are capable of anything. Why don't we go down and take a look? They won't get a chance to cut ours. I'll have the men fully armed and ready."

"The Captain thinks they may have been wiped out by galloping gangrene or something," the Ambassador informed. "Do you want to catch it?"

"Who? Me?" Shelton was horrified. "Good God, no!"

"Neither do I. So we're taking no chances."

"We're giving this world a miss?"

"That's right."

"Good. I'd hate my troops to be decimated without firing a shot."

"But it's all right so long as they have fired a shot?" Grayder inquired.

"You know what I mean. They're supposed to die in battle."

"They're having a run of hard luck," observed Grayder.

Shelton took a poor view of that remark and departed miffed.

The Ambassador said, "Why do you and the Colonel pick on each other from time to time?"

"He's army and I'm navy, Your Excellency. It's traditional."

"Is that so? Then it's a wonder you've not got worlds of your own." He took another useless look outside, went on, "I suppose we'd better signal the news about this dump. I'll get busy and write a report. Immediately it's been transmitted we might as well continue on our way."

"There's nothing to be gained by hanging around, Your Excellency."

"What's the next place?"

Grayder consulted his book. "Referred to only as K229. Its name is not known. Should be a suitable headquarters for you, I think."

"Why?"

"A large number went there. About four millions. That should have given them quite a head start. It ought to be the best developed planet of the lot."

"I'm not so sure. It depends on what they regard as development," opined the Ambassador. "Some of them have weird ideas of where to go and how to go there." Suspicion crept into his fat features. "What sort of lunatics were they?"

"Don't know, Your Excellency. It's the only planet about which the ancient records aren't specific. The colonists are described as assorted dissidents, whatever that means."

"Not as political rebels or incurable morons or religious cultists or anything like that?"

"No—just dissidents."

"It implies that the planet was confiscated by a disorganized rabble. Doesn't seem plausible to me. They couldn't have been widely assorted else they'd have chopped each other to pieces in jig time. They must have had something in common, something strong enough to create unity of purpose."

Grayder shrugged. "Hope of heaven and fear of hell is enough for some folk."

"I'm not frantic with delight over the artificial heavens we've seen so far. And there's much to be said for the so-called Terran hell in spite of all its shortcomings." Emitting a snort of disgust, the Ambassador reached for his pen. "I'll do this report. There's not much to say, thank goodness. Ain't nobody here but us corpses."

"Right," said Grayder. "We'll boost onward immediately you've finished."

The fourth and last planet was the third of ten circling a Sol-type sun. In size, mass, distance from primary and general appearance it was remarkably like Terra, differing only in that it had a little more land, a little less ocean. Ice-caps slightly smaller than Terra's gleamed at the north and south poles. Cloud formations straggled across land and seas. There was one large moon.

"Now this looks a lot more like home," approved the Ambassador. "And if after we've landed it feels the same way I'm having it for myself. The consuls are welcome to the loonier places."

"The only consul in this sector is the fellow we left on Hygeia," Grayder pointed out.

Taking no notice, the Ambassador enthused, "One moon. One ordinary moon of about the proper size. That's what I like to see. Half a dozen tiny ones racing each other through the night are too strong a reminder that one is umpteen millions of miles from anywhere. But with the right scenery, the right atmosphere and one moon I could imagine I'm on Terra. I only hope that the people have gained a modicum of plain hoss-sense and learned to behave themselves like decent Terrans."

"That I doubt," said Grayder.

"So do I. However, a reasonable approximation will come near enough to make me happy. So long as they're similar in all other respects they can hold voodoo ceremonies every Thursday afternoon for all I care."

He went silent as the ship closed in and the planet's dayside face rapidly expanded. Then followed the usual circling and photographing. A lot of villages and small towns were to be seen, also cultivated areas of large extent. It was obvious that this planet—while by no means fully exploited—was in the hands of colonists who were energetic and numerically strong.

Relieved that life was full, abundant and apparently free from alien disease, Grayder brought the ship down onto the first hard-standing he saw. Its enormous mass landed feather-like on a long, low hump amid well-tended fields. Again all the ports became filled with faces as everyone had a look at the new world.

The midway airlock opened, the gangway went down. As before, exit was made in strict order of precedence starting with the Ambassador and finishing with Sergeant Major Bidworthy. Grouping near the bottom of the gangway they spent the first few moments absorbing sunshine and fresh air.

His Excellency scuffled the thick turf under his feet, plucked a blade of it grunting as he stopped. He was so constructed that the effort came close to an athletic feat and gave him a crick in the belly.

"Eight-type grass. See that, Captain? Is it just a coincidence or did they bring seed with them?"

"Could be either. Several grassy worlds are known. And almost all colonists went away loaded with seeds."

"It's another touch of home, anyway. I think I'm going to like this place." The Ambassador gazed into the distance, doing it with pride of ownership. "Looks like there's someone working over there. He's using a little motor-cultivator with a pair of fat wheels. They can't be very backward, it seems. H'm-m-m!" He rubbed a couple of chins. "Bring him here. We'll have a talk and find out where it's best to make a start."

"Very well." Captain Grayder turned to Colonel Shelton. "His Excellency wishes to speak to that farmer." He pointed to the faraway figure.

"That farmer," said Shelton to Major Hame. "His Excellency wants him at once."

"Bring that farmer here," Hame ordered Lieutenant Deacon, "Quickly."

"Go get that farmer," Deacon told Sergeant Major Bidworthy. "And hurry—His Excellency is waiting."

Bidworthy sought around for a lesser rank, remembered that they were all inside, cleaning ship and not smoking, by his order. He, it seemed, was elected.

Tramping across four fields and coming within hailing distance of his objective, he performed a precise military halt, released a barracks square bellow of, "Hi, you!" and waved urgently.

The farmer stopped his steady trudging behind the tiny cultivator, wiped his forehead, glanced casually around. His indifferent manner suggested that the mountainous bulk of the ship was a mirage such as are five a penny around these parts. Bidworthy waved again, making it an authoritative summons. Now suddenly aware of the Sergeant Major's existence, the farmer calmly waved back, resumed his work.

Bidworthy employed a brief but pungeant expletive which—when its flames had died out—meant, "Dear me!" and marched fifty paces nearer. He could now see that the other was bushy-browed, leather-faced, tall and lean.

"Hi!" he bawled.

Stopping the cultivator again, the farmer leaned on one of its shafts and idly picked his teeth.

Smitten by the ingenious thought that perhaps during the last few centuries the old Terran language had been abandoned in favor of some other lingo, Bidworthy approached to within normal talking distance and asked, "Can you understand me?"

"Can any person understand another?" inquired the farmer with clear diction.

Bidworthy found himself afflicted with a moment of confusion. Recovering, he informed hurriedly, "His Excellency the Earth Ambassador wishes to speak with you at once."

"Is that so?" The other eyed him speculatively, had another pick at this teeth. "And what makes him excellent?"

"He is a person of considerable importance," said Bidworthy, unable to decide whether the other was trying to be funny at his expense or alternatively was what is known as a character. A lot of these long-isolated pioneering types liked to think of themselves as characters.

"Of considerable importance," echoed the farmer, narrowing his eyes at the horizon. He appeared to be trying to grasp a completely alien concept. After a while, he inquired, "What will happen to your home world when this person dies?"

"Nothing," Bidworthy admitted.

"It will roll on as before?"

"Yes."

"Round and round the sun?"

"Of course."

"Then," declared the farmer flatly, "if his existence or nonexistence makes no difference he cannot be important." With that, his little engine went *chuff-chuff* and the cultivator rolled forward.

Digging his nails into the palms of his hands, Bidworthy spent half a minute gathering oxygen before he said in hoarse tones, "Are you going to speak to the Ambassador or not?"

"Not."

"I cannot return without at least a message for His Excellency."

"Indeed?" The other was incredulous. "What is to stop you?" Then, noticing the alarming increase in Bidworthy's color, he added with compassion, "Oh, well, you may tell him that I said"—he paused while he thought it over—"God bless you and good-bye."

Sergeant Major Bidworthy was a powerful man who weighed more than two hundred pounds, had roamed the cosmos for twenty-five years and feared nothing. He had never been known to permit the shiver of one hair—but he was trembling all over by the time he got back to the base of the gangway.

His Excellency fastened a cold eye upon him and demanded, "Well?"

"He refuses to come." Bidworthy's veins stood out on his forehead. "And, sir, if only I could have him in the space troops for a few months I'd straighten him up and teach him to move at the double."

"I don't doubt that, Sergeant Major," the Ambassador soothed. He continued in a whispered aside to Colonel Shelton. "He's a good fellow but no diplomat. Too abrupt and harsh-voiced. Better go yourself and fetch that farmer. We can't loaf around forever waiting to learn where to begin."

"Very well, Your Excellency." Trudging across the field, Shelton caught up with the farmer, smiled pleasantly and said, "Good morning, my man."

Stopping his machine, the farmer sighed as if it were one of those days one has sometimes. His eyes were dark brown, almost black as they regarded the newcomer.

"What makes you think I'm *your* man?"

"It is a figure of speech," explained Shelton. He could see what was wrong now. Bidworthy had fallen foul of an irascible type. They'd been like two dogs snarling at one another. Oh, well, as a high-ranking officer he was competent to handle anybody, the good and the bad, the sweet and the sour, the jovial and the liverish. Shelton went on oilily, "I was only trying to be courteous."

"It must be said," meditated the farmer, "that that is something worth trying for—if you can make it."

Pinking a little, Shelton continued with determination, "I am commanded to request the pleasure of your company at the ship."

"Commanded?"

"Yes."

"Really and truly commanded?"

"Yes."

The other appeared to wander into a momentary daydream before he came back and asked blandly, "Think they'll get any pleasure out of my company?"

"I'm sure of it," said Shelton.

"You're a liar," said the farmer.

His color deepening, Colonel Shelton snapped, "I do not permit people to call me a liar."

"You've just permitted it," the farmer pointed out.

Letting it pass, Shelton insisted, "Are you coming to the ship?"

"No."

"Why not?"

"Myob!" said the farmer.

"What was that?"

"Myob!" he repeated. It sounded like some sort of insult.

Shelton went back, told the Ambassador, "That fellow is one of those too-clever types. At the finish all I could get out of him was 'Myob' whatever that mans."

"Local slang," chipped in Grayder. "An awful lot of it develops in four centuries. I've come across one or two worlds where there has been so much of it that to all intents and purposes it formed a new language."

"He understood your speech?" asked the Ambassador of Shelton.

"Yes, Your Excellency. And his own is quite good. But he won't leave his work." He reflected briefly, suggested, "If it were left to me I'd bring him in by force with an armed escort."

"That would encourage him to give essential information," commented the Ambassador with open sarcasm. He patted his stomach, smoothed his jacket, glanced down at his glossy shoes. "Nothing for it but to go and speak to him myself."

Shelton was shocked. "Your Excellency, you can't do *that!*"

"Why can't I?"

"It would be undignified."

"I am fully aware of the fact," said the Ambassador dryly. "What alternative do you suggest?"

"We can send out a patrol to find someone more coöperative."

"Someone better informed, too," Captain Grayder offered. "At best we won't get much out of one surly hayseed. I doubt whether he knows one quarter of what we require to learn."

"All right." The Ambassador dropped the idea of doing his own chores. "Organize a patrol and let's have some results."

"A patrol," said Colonel Shelton to Major Hame. "Nominate one immediately."

"Call out a patrol," Hame ordered Lieutenant Deacon. "At once."

"Parade a patrol forthwith, Sergeant Major," said Deacon.

Bidworthy lumbered up the gangway, stuck his head into the airlock and shouted, "Sergeant Gleed, out with your squad and make it snappy!" He gave a suspicious sniff and went farther into the lock. His voice gained several more decibels. "Who's been smoking? By heavens, if I catch the man——"

Across the fields something quietly went *chuff-chuff* while fat wheels crawled along.

The patrol formed by the right in two ranks of eight men each, turned at a barked command and marched off in the general direction of the ship's nose. They moved with perfect rhythm if no great beauty of motion. Their boots thumped in unison, their accoutrements clattered with martial noises and the orange-colored sun made sparkles on their metal.

Sergeant Gleed did not have to take his men far. They were one hundred yards behind the ship's great snout when he noticed a man ambling across the field to his right. Treating the ship with utter indifference, this character was making toward the farmer still toiling far over to the left.

"Patrol, right wheel!" yelled Gleed, swift to take advantage of the situation. The patrol right-wheeled, marched straight past the wayfarer who couldn't be bothered even to wave a handkerchief at them. Now Gleed ordered an about-turn and followed it with a take-him gesture.

Speeding up its pace, the patrol opened its ranks and became a double file of men tramping on either side of the long pedestrian. Ignoring his suddenly acquired escort the latter continued to plod straight ahead like one long convinced that all is illusion.

"Left wheel!" roared Gleed, trying to bend the whole caboodle towards the waiting Ambassador.

Swiftly obedient, the double file headed leftward, one, two, three, hup! It was neat, precise execution beautiful to watch. Only one thing spoiled it: the man in the middle stubbornly maintained his self-chosen orbit and ambled casually between numbers four and five of the right-hand file.

That upset Gleed, especially since the patrol continued to thump steadily ambassadorwards for lack of a further order. His Excellency was being treated to the unmilitary spectacle of an escort dumbly boot-beating one way while its prisoner airily mooched another way. In due course Colonel Shelton would have plenty to say about it and anything he forgot Bidworthy would remember.

"Patrol!" hoarsed Gleed, pointing an outraged finger at the escapee and momentarily dismissing all regulation commands from his mind, "Get that mug!"

Breaking ranks, they moved at the double and surrounded the wanderer too closely to permit further progress. Perforce he stopped.

Gleed came up and said somewhat breathlessly, "Look, the Earth Ambassador wants to speak to you—that's all."

The other gazed at him with mild blue eyes. He was a funny-looking sample, long overdue for a shave. He had a fringe of ginger whiskers sticking out all around his face and bore faint resemblance to a sunflower.

"I should care," he said.

"Are you going to talk with His Excellency?" Gleed persisted.

"Naw." The other nodded toward the farmer. "Going to talk to Zeke."

"The Ambassador first," retorted Gleed, wearing his tough expression. "He's a big noise."

"I don't doubt that," remarked the sunflower, showing what sort of a noise he had in mind.

"Smartie Artie, eh?" grated Gleed, pushing his face close and making it unpleasant. He signed to his men. "All right, hustle him along. We'll show him!"

Smartie Artie chose this moment to sit down. He did it sort of solidly, giving himself the aspect of a squatting statue solidly anchored for the remainder of eternity. But Gleed had handled sitters before, the only difference being that this one was cold sober.

"Pick him up," commanded Gleed, "and carry him."

So they picked him up and carried him, feet first, whiskers last. He hung limp and unresisting in their hands, a dead weight made as difficult as possible to bear. In this inauspicious manner he arrived in the presence of the Ambassador where the escort plonked him on his feet.

Promptly he set out for Zeke.

"Hold him, darn you!" howled Gleed.

The patrol grabbed and clung tight. The Ambassador eyed the whiskers with well-bred concealment of distaste, coughed delicately and spoke.

"I am truly sorry that you had to come to me in this fashion."

"In that case," suggested the prisoner, "you could have saved yourself some mental anguish by not permitting it to happen."

"There was no other choice. We've got to make contact somehow."

"I don't see it," said Ginger Whiskers. "What's so special about this date?"

"The date?" The Ambassador frowned in puzzlement. "What has the date got to do with it?"

"That's exactly what I'm asking."

"The point eludes me." The Ambassador turned to the others. "Do you understand what he's aiming at?"

Shelton said, "I can hazard a guess, Your Excellency. I think he is hinting that since we've left them without contact for four hundred years there is no particular urgency about making it today." He looked to the sunflower for confirmation.

That worthy rallied to his support by remarking, "You're doing pretty well for a halfwit."

Regardless of Shelton's own reaction, this was too much for Bidworthy purpling nearby. His chest came up and his eyes caught fire. His voice was an authoritative rasp.

"Be more respectful while addressing high-ranking officers!"

The prisoner's mild blue eyes turned upon him in childish amazement, examined him slowly from feet to head and all the way down again. The eyes drifted back inquiringly to the Ambassador.

"Who is this preposterous person?"

Dismissing the question with an impatient wave of his hand, the Ambassador said, "See here, it is not our purpose to bother you from sheer perversity, as you seem to think. Neither do we wish to detain you any longer than is necessary. All we——"

Pulling at his face-fringe as if to accentuate its offensiveness, the other interjected, "It being you, of course, who determines the length of the necessity?"

"On the contrary, you may decide that for yourself," gave back the Ambassador, displaying admirable self-control. "All you need do is tell us——"

"Then I've decided it right now," the prisoner chipped in. He tried to heave himself free of his escort. "Let me go talk to Zeke."

"All you need do," the Ambassador persisted, "is tell us where we can find a local official who can put us into touch with your central government." His gaze was stern, commanding, as he added, "For instance, where is the nearest police post?"

"Myob!" said Ginger Whiskers.

"What was that?"

"Myob!"

"The same to you," retorted the Ambassador, his patience evaporating.

"That's precisely what I'm trying to do," insisted the prisoner, enigmatically. "Only you won't let me do it."

"If I may make a suggestion, Your Excellency," put in Shelton, "allow me——"

"I require no suggestions and I won't allow you," said the Ambassador, somewhat out of temper. "I have had enough of all this stupid tomfoolery. I think we have landed at random in an area reserved for imbeciles. It would be as well to recognize the fact and get out of it with no more delay."

"Now you're talking," approved Ginger Whiskers. "And the farther the better."

"We have no intention of leaving this planet, if that is what's in your incomprehensible mind," asserted the Ambassador. He stamped a proprietory foot into the turf. "This is part of the Terran Empire. As such it is going to be recognized, charted and organized."

"Heah, heah!" put in the senior civil servant who aspired to honors in elocution.

His Excellency threw a frown behind, went on, "We'll move the shop to some other section where brains are brighter." He turned attention to the escort. "Let him go. Probably he is in a hurry to borrow a razor."

They released their grips. Ginger Whiskers at once turned toward the distant farmer much as if he were a magnetized needle irresistibly drawn Zekeward. Without another word he set off at his original slovenly pace. Disappointment and disgust showed on the faces of Bidworthy and Gleed as they watched him depart.

"Have the vessel shifted at once, Captain," the Ambassador said to Grayder. "Plant it near to a likely town—not out in the wilds where every yokel views strangers as a bunch of crooks."

He marched importantly up the gangway. Captain Grayder followed, then Colonel Shelton, then the elocutionist. Next their successors in correct order of precedence. Lastly, Gleed and his men.

The airlock closed. The warning siren sounded. Despite its immense bulk the ship shivered briefly from end to end and soared without deafening uproar or spectacular display of flame.

Indeed, there was silence save for a little engine going *chuff-chuff* and the murmurings of the two men walking behind it. Neither took the trouble to look around to see what was happening.

"Seven pounds of prime tobacco is a heck of a lot to give for one case of brandy," Ginger Whiskers protested.

"Not for my brandy," said Zeke. "It's stronger than a thousand Gands and smoother than an Earthman's downfall."

8

The great ship's next touchdown was made on a wide flat about two miles north of a town estimated to hold twelve to fifteen thousand people. Grayder would have preferred to survey the place from low altitude before making his landing but one cannot handle a huge space-going vessel as if it were an atmospheric tug. Only two things can be done when so close to a planetary surface—the ship is taken straight up or brought straight down with no room for fiddling betweentimes.

So Grayder dumped the ship in the best spot he could find when finding is a matter of split-second decisions. It made a rut only ten feet deep, the ground being hard with a rock bed. The gangway was shoved out. The procession descended in the same order as before.

Casting an anticipatory look toward the town, the Ambassador registered irritation. "Something is badly out of kilter here. There's the town not so far away. Here we are in plain view with a ship like a metal mountain. At least a thousand people must have seen us coming down even if all the rest are holding séances behind drawn curtains or playing poker in the cellars. Are they interested? Are they excited?"

"It doesn't seem so," contributed Shelton, pulling industriously at an eyelid for the sake of feeling it spring back.

"I wasn't asking you. I am telling you. They are not excited. They are not surprised. They are not even interested. One would almost think they'd had a ship here that was full of smallpox or that swindled them out of something. What's wrong with them?"

"Possibly they lack curiosity," Shelton ventured.

"Either that or they're afraid. Or maybe the entire gang of them is more cracked than any bunch on any other world. Practically all these planets were appropriated by dotty people who wanted to establish a haven where their eccentricities could run loose. And nutty notions become conventional after four hundred years of undisturbed continuity. It is then considered normal and proper to nurse the bats out of your grandfather's attic. That and generations of inbreeding can create some queer types. But we'll cure them before we're through."

"Yes, Your Excellency, most certainly we will."

"You don't look so well-balanced yourself, chasing that eyelid around your face," reproved the Ambassador. He pointed south-east as Shelton stuck the fidgety hand firmly into a pocket. "There's a road over there. Wide and well-built by the looks of it. They don't construct such a highway for the mere fun of it. Ten to one it's an important artery."

"That's how it looks to me," Shelton agreed.

"Put that patrol across it, Colonel. If your men don't bring in a willing talker within reasonable time we'll send the entire battalion into the town itself."

"A patrol," said Shelton to Major Hame.

"Call out the patrol," Hame ordered Lieutenant Deacon.

"That patrol again, Sergeant Major," said Deacon.

Bidworthy raked out Gleed and his men, indicated the road, barked a bit and shooed them on their way.

They marched, Gleed in front. Their objective was half a mile away and angled toward the town. The left-hand file had a clear view of the nearest suburbs, eyed the buildings wistfully, wished Gleed in warmer regions with Bidworthy stoking the hell-fire beneath him.

Hardly had they reached their goal than a customer appeared. He came from the town's outskirts, zooming along at fast pace on a contraption vaguely like a motorcycle. It ran on a big pair of rubber balls and was pulled by a caged fan. Gleed spread his men across the road.

The oncomer's machine slddenly gave forth a harsh, penetrating sound that reminded everybody of Bidworthy in the presence of dirty boots.

"Stay put," warned Gleed. "I'll skin the fellow who gives way and leaves a gap."

Again the shrill metallic warning. Nobody moved. The machine slowed, came up to them at a crawl and stopped. Its fan continued to spin at slow rate, the blades almost visible and giving out a steady hiss.

"What's the idea?" demanded the rider. He was lean-featured, in his middle thirties, wore a gold ring in his nose and had a pigtail four feet long.

Blinking incredulously at this get-up, Gleed managed to jerk an indicative thumb toward the metal mountain and say,

"Earth ship."

"Well, what do you expect me to do about it?—throw a fit of hysterics?"

"We expect you to coöperate," informed Gleed, still bemused by the pigtail. He had never seen such a thing before. It was in no way effeminate, he decided. Rather did it lend a touch of ferocity like that worn—according to the picture book—by certain North American aborigines in the dim and distant past.

"Coöperation," mused the rider. "Now there is a beautiful word. You know exactly what it means, of course?"

"I'm not a dope."

"The precise degree of your idiocy is not under discussion at the moment," the rider pointed out. His nose-ring waggled a bit as he spoke. "We are talking about coöperation. I take it you do quite a lot of it yourself?"

"You bet I do," Gleed assured. "And so does everyone else who knows what's good for him."

"Let's keep to the subject, shall we? Let's not sidetrack and go rambling all over the conversational map." He revved up his fan a little then let it slow down again. "You are given orders and you obey them?"

"Of course. I'd have a rough time if——"

"That is what you call coöperation?" put in the other. He hunched his shoulders, pursed his bottom lip. "Well, it's nice to check the facts of history. The books *could* be wrong." His fan flashed into a circle of light and the machine surged forward. "Pardon me."

The front rubber ball barged forcefully between two men, knocking them aside without injury. With a high whine the machine shot down the road, its fan-blast making its rider's plaited hairdo point horizontally backward.

"You substandard morons!" raged Gleed as the pair got up and dusted themselves. "I told you to stand fast. What d'you mean by letting him run out on us like that?"

"Didn't have much choice about it, Sarge," answered one surlily.

"I want none of your back-chat. You could have busted one of his balloons if you'd had your guns ready. That would have stopped him."

"You didn't tell us to use our guns."

"Where was your own, anyway?" added a sneaky voice.

Gleed whirled on the others and demanded, "Who said that?" His eyes raked a long row of impassive faces. It was impossible to detect the culprit. "I'll shake you up with the next quota of fatigues," he promised. "I'll see to it that——"

"The Sergeant Major's coming," one of them warned.

Bidworthy was four hundred yards away and making martial progress towards them. Arriving in due time, he cast a cold, contemptuous glance over the patrol.

"What happened?"

"Giving me a lot of lip, he was," complained Gleed after providing a brief account of the incident. "He looked like one of those Chickasaws with an oil well."

"Did he really?" Bidworthy surveyed him a moment, then invited, "And what is a Chickasaw?"

"I read about them somewhere once when I was a kid," explained Gleed, happy to bestow a modicum of learning. "They got rich on oil. They had long, plaited haircuts, wore blankets and rode around in gold-plated automobiles."

"Sounds crazy to me," said Bidworthy. "I gave up all that magic-carpet stuff when I was seven. I was deep in ballistics before I was twelve and military logistics when I was fourteen." He sniffed loudly and gave the other a jaundiced eye. "Some guys suffer from arrested development."

"They actually existed," Gleed maintained. "They——"

"So did fairies," snapped Bidworthy. "My mother said so. My mother was a good woman. She didn't tell me a lot of goddam lies—often." He spat on the road. "Be your age!" Then he glowered at the patrol. "All right, get out your guns—assuming that you've got them and know where they are and which hand to hold them in. Take orders from me. I'll deal personally with the next character who comes along."

Sitting on a large rock by the roadside, he planted an expectant gaze on the town. Gleed posed near him, slightly pained. The patrol remained strung across the road with guns held ready. Half an hour crawled by without anything happening.

One of the men pleaded, "Can we smoke, Sergeant Major?"

"No!"

They fell into lugubrious silence, licking their lips from time to time and doing plenty of thinking. They had lots about which to think. A town—any town of human occupation—had desirable features not to be found anywhere else in the cosmos. Lights, company, freedom, laughter, all the makings of life. And one can go hungry too long.

Eventually a large coach emerged from the town's outskirts, hit the high road and came bowling towards them. A long, shiny, streamlined job, it rolled on twenty balls in two rows of ten, gave forth a whine similar to but louder than that of the motorcycle, and had no visible fans. It was loaded with people.

At a point two hundred yards from the road-block a loud-speaker under the vehicle's bonnet blared an urgent, "Make way! Make way!"

"This is it," commented Bidworthy with much satisfaction. "We've caught a dollop of them. One of them is going to confess or I'll resign from the space service." He got off his rock and stood in readiness.

"Make way! Make way!"

"Perforate his balloons if he tries to bull his way through," ordered Bidworthy.

It wasn't necessary. The coach lost pace, stopped with its bonnet a yard from the waiting file. Its driver appeared out of the side of his cab. Other faces snooped curiously farther back.

Composing himself and determined to try the effect of fraternal cordiality, Bidworthy went up to the driver and said with great difficulty, "Good morning!"

"Your time-sense is shot to pot," responded the other ungratefully. He had a heavy blue jowl, a broken nose, cauliflower ears and looked the sort who usually drives with others in hot and vengeful pursuit. "Can't you afford a watch?"

"Eh?"

"It isn't morning. It's late afternoon."

"So it is," admitted Bidworthy, forcing a cracked smile. "Good afternoon!"

"I'm not so sure about that," mused the driver, leaning on his steering-wheel and moodily scratching his head. "We get an afternoon in every day. It's always the same. Morning goes and what happens? You're stuck with an afternoon. I've become hardened to it. And this one is just another nearer the grave."

"That may be," conceded Bidworthy, little struck with this ghoulish angle, "but I have other things to worry about and——"

"Fat lot of use worrying about anything, past, present or whatever," advised the driver. "Because there are far bigger worries to come. Stick around long enough and you'll have some real stinkers in your lap."

"Perhaps so," said Bidworthy, inwardly feeling that this was a poor time to contemplate the darker side of existence. "But I prefer to deal with my own troubles in my own way."

"Nobody's troubles are entirely their own, nor their methods of coping," continued the tough-looking oracle. "Are they now?"

"I don't know and I don't care," growled Bidworthy, his composure thinning down as his blood pressure built up. He was irefully conscious of Gleed and the patrol watching, listening and probably grinning like stupid apes behind his back. There was also the load of gaping passengers. "I think you're talking just to stall me. You might as well know that it won't work. I'm here for a purpose and that purpose is going to be served. The Terran Ambassador is waiting——"

"So are we," emphasized the driver.

"He wants to speak to you," Bidworthy went stubbornly on, "and he's going to speak to you."

"I'd be the last to prevent him. We've got free speech here. Let him step up and say his piece so that we can go our way."

"*You*," informed Bidworthy, "are going to *him*." He signed to the rest of the coach. "The whole lot of you."

"Not me," denied a fat man sticking his head out of a side window. He wore thick-lensed glasses that made his eyes look like poached eggs. Moreover, he was adorned with a tall hat candy-striped in white and pink. "Not me," repeated this vision with considerable firmness.

"Me neither," supported the driver.

"All right." Bidworthy displayed maximum menace. "Move this birdcage one inch backward or forward and we'll shoot your pot-bellied tires to thin strips. Get out of that cab."

"Ha-ha. I'm too comfortable. Try fetching me."

Bidworthy beckoned to the nearest six men. "You heard him—take him up on that."

Tearing open the cab door, they grabbed. If they had expected the victim to put up a futile fight against heavy odds, they were disappointed. He made no attempt to resist. They got him, lugged together and he yielded with good grace. His body leaned to one side and came halfway out of the door.

That was as far as they could get him.

"Come on," urged Bidworthy, showing impatience. "Heave him loose. You don't have to be feeble. Show him who's who. He isn't a fixture."

One of the men climbed over the body, poked around inside the cab and announced, "He is, you know."

"What d'you mean?"

"He's chained to the steering column."

"Nonsense. Let me see." He had a look and found that it was so. A chain and a small but heavy and complicated padlock linked the driver's leg to his coach. "Where's the key?"

"Search me," invited the driver.

They did just that. The effort proved futile. No key.

".Who's got it?"

"Myob!"

"Shove him back into his seat," ordered Bidworthy, looking savage. "We'll take the passengers. One yap is as good as another so far as I'm concerned." Striding to the doors, he jerked them open. "All out and make it snappy."

Nobody budged. They studied him silently, with various expressions not one of which did anything to help his ego. The fat man with the candy striped hat mooned at him sardonically. Bidworthy decided that he did not like the fat man and that a stiff course of military calisthenics might thin him down a bit.

"You can come out on your feet," he suggested to the passengers in general and the fat man in particular, "or on your necks. Whichever you prefer. Make up your minds."

"If you can't use your head you can at least use your eyes," commented the fat man happily. He shifted in his seat to the accompaniment of metallic clanking noises.

Bidworthy accepted the idea, leaning through the doors for a better look. Then he clambered into the vehicle, went its full length while carefully studying each passenger. His florid features were two shades darker when he emerged and spoke to Sergeant Gleed.

"They are all chained. Every one of them." He glared at the driver. "What's the purpose of manacling the lot?"

"Myob!" said the driver airily.

"Who has the keys?"

"Myob!"

Taking a deep breath, Bidworthy declaimed to nobody in particular, "Every once in a while I hear of somebody running amok and laying them out by the dozens. I've always wondered why—but now I know." He gnawed his knuckles, added to Gleed, "We can't run this contraption to the ship with that dummy blocking the controls. Either we must find the keys or get tools and cut them loose."

"Or you could wave us on our way and then go take a pill," offered the driver.

"Shut up! If I'm stuck here another million years I'll see to it that——"

"Here's the Colonel," muttered Gleed, giving him a nudge.

Colonel Shelton arrived, walked once slowly and officiously around the outside of the coach, examined its construction and weighed up its occupants. He flinched at the striped hat whose owner leered at him through the glass. Then he came over to the disgruntled group.

"What's the trouble this time, Sergeant Major?"

"They're as crazy as all the others, sir. They're full of impudence and say, 'Myob' and couldn't care less about His Excellency. They don't want to come out and we can't make them because they're chained in their seats."

"Chained?" Shelton's eyebrows lifted halfway toward his hair. "What on earth for?"

"I don't know, sir. All I can tell you is that they're fastened in like a bunch of gangsters being hauled to the pokey and——"

Shelton moved off without waiting to hear the rest. He had a look for himself, came back.

"You may have something there, Sergeant Major. But I don't think they are criminals."

"No, sir?"

"No." He threw a significant glance towards the fat man's colorful headgear and several other sartorial eccentricities including a ginger-haired individual's foot-wide polka-dotted bow. "It's more likely they're a consignment of lunatics being taken to an asylum. I'll ask the driver." Going to the cab, he said, "Do you mind telling me your destination?"

"Yes," responded the other.

"Very well, where is it?"

"Look," said the driver, "are we talking the same language?"

"Eh? Why?"

"You've just asked me whether I mind and I said yes." He made a disparaging gesture. "I do mind."

"You refuse to tell?"

"Your aim's improving, Sonny."

"Sonny?" put in Bidworthy, vibrant with outrage. "Do you realize that you are speaking to a colonel?"

"What's a colonel?" asked the driver interestedly.

"By hokey, if you——"

"Leave this to me," insisted Shelton, waving the furious Bidworthy down. His expression was cold as he returned attention to the driver. "On your way. I'm sorry you've been detained."

"Think nothing of it," said the driver with exaggerated politeness. "I'll do as much for you some day."

With that enigmatic remark he let his machine roll forward. The patrol parted to make room. Building up its whine to the top note, the coach sped down the road and diminished into the dusty distance.

"This planet," swore Bidworthy, staring purple-faced after it, "has more no-good bums in need of discipline than any place this side of—"

"Calm yourself, Sergeant Major," urged Shelton. "I feel exactly the same way as you do—but I'm taking care of my arteries. Blowing them full of bumps like seaweed won't solve any problems."

"Maybe so, sir, but—"

"We're up against something mighty peculiar here," Shelton went on. "We've got to find out precisely what it is and how best to cope with it. In all probability it means we'll have to devise new tactics. So far the patrol has achieved nothing. It is wasting its time. Obviously we'll have to concoct a more effective method of getting into touch with the powers-that-be. March the men back to the ship, Sergeant Major."

"Very well, sir." Bidworthy saluted, swung around, clicked his heels, opened a cavernous mouth. "Patro-o-ol . . . right form!"

Aboard ship the resulting conference lasted well into the night and halfway through the following morning. During these argumentative hours various oddments of traffic, mostly vehicular, passed along the road. But nothing paused to view the monster spaceship, nobody approached for a friendly word with its crew. The strange inhabitants of this world seemed to be afflicted with a local form of mental blindness, unable to see a thing until it was thrust into their faces and then surveying it squint-eyed.

One passer-by in mid-morning was a long, low truck whining on two dozen balls and loaded with girls wearing bright head-scarves. The girls were tunefully singing something about one little kiss before we part, dear. A number of troops loafing near the gangway came eagerly to life, waved, whistled and yoohooed. Their effort was a total waste for the singing continued without break or pause and nobody waved back.

To add to the discomfiture of the love-hungry, Bidworthy stuck his head out of the airlock and rasped, "If you monkeys are bursting with surplus energy I can find a few jobs for you to do—nice, dirty ones." He seared them one at a time before he withdrew.

Up near the ship's nose the top brass sat around the chartroom's horseshoe table and debated the situation. Most of them were content to repeat with extra emphasis what they had said the previous evening, there being no new points to bring up.

"Are you certain," the Ambassador asked Grayder, "that this planet has not been visited since the last emigration transport dumped its final load four centuries ago?"

"I'm quite positive, Your Excellency. Any such visit would be on record."

"Yes, if made by a Terran ship. But what about others? I feel it in my bones that at some time or other these people have fallen foul of one or more vessels calling unofficially and been leery of spaceships ever since. Perhaps somebody got tough with them and tried to muscle in where he wasn't wanted. Or perhaps they've had to beat off a gang of pirates. Or maybe they've been swindled by unscrupulous traders."

"Absolutely impossible, Your Excellency," declared Grayder, suppressing a smile. "Emigration was so widely scattered over so large a number of worlds that even today every one of them is under-populated, under-developed and utterly unable to build spaceships of any kind no matter how rudimentary. Some may have the technical know-how but they lack the industrial facilities, of which they need plenty."

"Yes, that is what I've always understood."

Grayder went on, "All Blieder-drive vessels are built in the system of Sol and registered as Terran ships. Complete track is kept of their movements and their whereabouts are always known. The only other spaceships in existence are eighty or ninety antiquated rocket jobs bought at scrap price by the Epsilon system for haulage work between its fourteen closely-spaced planets. An old-fashioned rocket-ship couldn't reach this world in a hundred years."

"No, of course not."

"Unofficial boats capable of this long range just don't exist," Grayder assured. "Neither do space buccaneers and for much the same reason. A Blieder-drive ship is so costly that a would-be pirate would have to be a billionaire to become a pirate."

"Then," said the Ambassador heavily, "back we go to my original theory; that a lot of inbreeding has made them crazier than their colonizing ancestors."

"There's plenty to be said in favor of that idea," put in Shelton. "You should have seen the coach-load I looked over. There was a fellow like a bankrupt mortician wearing odd shoes, one brown and one a repulsive yellow. Also a moon-faced gump sporting a hat apparently made from the skin of a barber's pole, all stripy." With a sad attempt at wit, he finished, "The only thing missing was his bubble-pipe—and probably he'll be given that when he arrives."

"Arrives where?"

"I don't know, Your Excellency. They refused to tell us where they were going."

Giving him a satirical look, the Ambassador remarked, "Well, that is a valuable addition to the sum total of our knowledge. Our minds are now enriched by the thought that an anonymous individual may be presented with a futile object for an indefinable purpose when he reaches his unknown destination."

Shelton subsided wishing that he had never seen the fat man or, for that matter, the fat man's cockeyed world.

"Somewhere they've got a capital, a civic seat, a center of government wherein function the people who hold all the strings," the Ambassador asserted. "We've got to find that place before we can take over and reorganize on up-to-date lines. A capital is big by the standards of its own administrative area. It is never an ordinary, nondescript place. It has obvious physical features giving it importance above the average. It should be easily visible from the air. We must make a systematic search for it—in fact that's what we should have done in the first place. Other planets' capital cities have been identified without trouble. What's the hoodoo on this one?"

"See for yourself, Your Excellency." Grayder poked several photographs across the table. "The situation is rather similar to that on Hygeia. You can see the two hemispheres quite clearly. They reveal nothing resembling a superior city. There isn't even a town conspicuously larger than its fellows or possessing enough outstanding features to set it apart from the others."

"I don't put great faith in pictures especially when taken at high speed or great altitude. The naked eye always can see more. We've got four lifeboats that should be able to search this world from pole to pole. Why don't we use them?"

"Because, Your Excellency, they were not designed for such a purpose."

"Does that matter so long as they get results?"

Patiently, Grayder explained, "They were built to be launched in free space and to hit up forty thousand miles an hour. They are ordinary, old-style rocket-ships to be used only in a grave emergency."

"Well, what of it?"

"It is not possible to make efficient ground-survey with the naked eye at any speed in excess of about four hundred miles per hour. Keep the lifeboats down to that and you'd be trying to fly them at landing-speed, muffling their tubes, balling up their motors, creating a terrible waste of fuel and inviting a crash which you're likely to get before you're through."

"Then," commented the Ambassador, "it is high time we had Blieder-drive lifeboats on Blieder-drive ships."

"I couldn't agree more, Your Excellency. But the smallest Blieder apparatus has an Earth-mass of more than three hundred tons. That's far too much for little boats." Picking up the photographs, Grayder slid them into a drawer. "The trouble with us is that everything we've got moves a heck of a lot too fast. What we really need is an ancient, propeller-driven airplane. It could do something that we can't—it could go slow."

"You might as well yearn for a bicycle," scoffed the Ambassador, feeling thwarted.

"We have a bicycle," Grayder informed. "Tenth Engineer Harrison owns one."

"And he has actually brought it with him?"

"It goes everywhere he goes. There's a rumor that he sleeps with it."

"A spaceman toting a bicycle!" The Ambassador blew his nose with a loud honk. "I take it that he is thrilled by the sense of immense velocity it gives him, an ecstatic feeling of rushing headlong through space?"

"I wouldn't know, Your Excellency."

"H'm! Bring this Harrison here. I'd like to see him. Perhaps we can set a crackpot to catch a crackpot."

Going to the caller-board, Grayder spoke over the ship's system. "Tenth Engineer Harrison will report to the chartroom at once."

Within ten minutes Harrison appeared, breathless and dishevelled. He had walked fast three-quarters of a mile from the Blieder room. He was thin and woebegone, expecting trouble. His ears were large enough to cut out the pedaling with the wind behind him and he wiggled them nervously as he faced the assembled officers. The Ambassador examined him with curiosity, much as a zoologist would inspect a pink giraffe.

"Mister, I understand that you possess a bicycle."

At once on the defensive, Harrison said, "There's nothing against it in the regulations, sir, and therefore——"

"Damn the regulations," swore the Ambassador. "Can you ride the thing?"

"Of course, sir."

"All right. We're stalled in the middle of a crazy situation and we're turning to crazy methods to get moving. Upon your ability and willingness to ride a bicycle the fate of an empire may stand or fall. Do you understand me, Mister?"

"I do, sir," said Harrison, unable to make head or tail of this.

"So I want you to do an extremely important job for me. I want you to get out your bicycle, ride into town, find the mayor, sheriff, grand panjandrum, supreme galootie or whatever he is called, and tell him that he is officially invited to evening dinner along with any other civic dignitaries he cares to bring. That, of course, includes their wives."

"Very well, sir."

"Informal attire," added the Ambassador.

Harrison jerked up one ear and dropped the other. "What was that, sir?"

"They can dress how they like."

"I get it. Do I go right now, sir?"

"At once. Return as quickly as you can and bring me the reply."

Saluting sloppily, Harrison went out. His Excellency found an easy-chair, reposed in it at full length, smiled with satisfaction.

"It's as easy as that." Pulling out a long cigar, he bit off its end. "If we can't touch their minds we'll appeal to their bellies." He cocked a knowing eye at Grayder. "Captain, see that there is plenty to drink. Strong stuff. Venusian cognac or something equally potent. Give them lots of hootch and an hour at a well-filled table and they'll talk all night. We won't be able to shut them up." He lit the cigar, puffed luxuriously. "That is the tried and trusted technique of high diplomacy—the insidious seduction of the distended gut. It always works. You'll see!"

9

Pedaling briskly down the road, Tenth Engineer Harrison reached the first street on either side of which were small detached houses with neat gardens back and front. A plump, amiable looking woman was trimming a hedge halfway along. He pulled up near to her, politely touched his cap.

"'Scuse me, ma'am, I'm looking for the biggest man in town."

She part-turned, gave him no more than a casual glance, pointed her clipping-shears southward. "That would be Jeff Baines. First on the right and second on the left. It's a small delicatessen."

"Thank you."

He moved on, hearing the steady *snip-snip* resume behind him. First on the right. He curved around a long, low, rubber-balled truck parked by the corner. Second on the left. Three children pointed at him dramatically and yelled shrill warnings that his back wheel was going round. He found the delicatessen, propped a pedal on the curb, gave his machine a reassuring pat before he went inside and had a look at Jeff.

There was plenty to see. Jeff had four chins, a twenty-two inch neck, and a paunch that stuck out half a yard. An ordinary mortal could have got into either leg of his pants without bothering to take off his diving suit. Jeff Baines weighed at least three hundred pounds and undoubtedly *was* the biggest man in town.

"Wanting something?" inquired Jeff, lugging it up from far down.

"Not exactly." Harrison eyed the succulent food display and decided that anything unsold by nightfall was not thrown out to the cats. "I'm looking for a certain person."

"Are you now? Usually I avoid that sort—but every man to his taste." He plucked a fat lip while he mused a moment, then suggested, "Try Sid Wilcock over on Dane Avenue. He's the most certain man I know."

"I didn't mean it that way," said Harrison. "I meant that I'm searching for somebody particular."

"Then why the blazes didn't you say so in the first place?" Jeff Baines worked over the new problem, finally offered, "Tod Green ought to fit that specification topnotch. You'll find him in the shoe-shop at the end of this road. He's particular enough for anyone. He's downright finicky."

"You persist in misunderstanding me," Harrison told him and then went on to make it plainer. "I'm hunting a local bigwig so that I can invite him to a feed."

Resting himself on a high stool which he overlapped by a foot all round, Jeff Baines eyed him peculiarly. "There's something lopsided about this. Indeed, it seems crazy to me."

"Why?"

"You're going to use up a considerable slice of your life finding a fellow who wears a wig, especially if you insist that it's got to be a big one. And then again, where's the point of dumping an ob on him merely because he uses a bean-blanket?"

"Eh?"

"It's plain horse-sense to plant an ob where it will cancel another one out, isn't it?"

"Is it?" Harrison let his mouth hang open while his mind struggled with the strange problem of how to plant an ob.

"So you don't know? You're exposing your tonsils and looking dopey because you don't know?" Jeff Baines massaged a couple of his chins and sighed. He pointed at the other's middle. "Is that a uniform you're wearing?"

"Yes."

"A genuine, pukka-dyed-in-the-wool uniform?"

"Of course."

"Ah," said Jeff. "That's where you've fooled me—coming here by yourself, on your ownsome. If there had been a gang of you dressed identically the same I'd have known at once that it was a uniform. That's what uniform means: all alike. Doesn't it?"

"I suppose so," agreed Harrison, who had never given it a thought.

"So you're from that ship. I ought to have guessed it in the beginning. I must be slow on the uptake today. But I didn't expect to see one, just one, messing around on a pedal contraption. It goes to show, doesn't it?"

"Yes," said Harrison, glancing warily backward to make sure that no opportunist had swiped his bicycle while he was engaged in conversation. "It goes to show."

"All right, let's have it. Why have you come here and what do you want?"

"I've been trying to tell you all along. I've been sent to—"

"Been sent?" Jeff's eyes widened a little. "Mean to say you actually let yourself be *sent*?"

Harrison gaped at him. "Of course. Why not?"

"Oh, I get it now," said Jeff, his puzzled features suddenly clearing. "You confuse me with the queer way you talk. What you really mean is that you planted an ob on somebody, eh?"

Desperately, Harrison asked, "For heaven's sake, what's an ob?"

"He doesn't know," commented Jeff Baines, looking prayerfully at the ceiling. "He doesn't even know *that!*" For a short while he contemplated the ignoramus with condescending pity before he said, "You hungry by any chance?"

"Going on that way."

"All right. I could tell you what an ob is. But I'll do something better—I'll show you." Heaving himself off the stool, he waddled to the door at the back. "God alone knows why I should bother to educate a uniform. It's just that I'm bored. C'mon, follow me."

Obediently, Harrison went behind the counter, paused to give his bicycle a reassuring nod, trailed the other through a passage and into a yard.

Jeff Baines pointed to a stack of cases. "Canned goods." He indicated an adjacent store. "Bust them open and pile the stuff in there. Stack the empties outside. Please yourself whether you do it or not. That's freedom, isn't it?" He lumbered back into the shop.

Left to himself, Harrison scratched his large ears and thought it over. Somewhere, he felt, there was an obscure sort of confidence trick. A candidate named Harrison was being tempted to qualify for his sucker certificate. But if the play was beneficial to its organizer it might be worth learning because it could then be passed on to other victims. One must speculate in order to accumulate.

So he dealt with the cases as required. It cost him twenty minutes of hard, slogging work after which he returned to the shop.

"Now," explained Baines, "you've done something for me. That means you've planted an ob on me. I don't thank you for what you have done. There's no need to. All I have to do is get rid of the ob."

"Ob?"

"Obligation. Why use a long word when a short one is plenty good enough? An obligation is an ob. I shift it this way: Seth Warburton, next door but one, has got half a dozen of my obs saddled on him. So I get rid of mine to you and relieve him of one of his to me by sending you around for a meal." He scribbled briefly on a slip of paper. "Give him this."

Harrison stared at it. In casual scrawl it read, "Feed this bum."

Slightly dazed, he wandered out, stood by his bicycle and again examined the paper. Bum, it said. He could think of several on the ship who'd explode with wrath at the sight of that. Then his attention drifted to the second shop farther along. It had a window crammed with comestibles and two big words on the sign-strip above: *Seth's Gulper.*

Coming to a decision which was encouraged by his insides, he walked into Seth's holding the paper as if it were a death warrant. Beyond the door there was a long counter, some steam and a clatter of crockery. He chose a seat at a marble-topped table occupied by a gray-eyed brunette.

"Do you mind?" he inquired politely as he lowered himself into the chair.

"Do I mind what?" She examined his ears as if they were curious phenomena. "Babies, dogs, aged relatives or standing around in the rain?"

"Do you mind me sitting here?"

"I can please myself whether or not I endure it. That's freedom, isn't it?"

"Yes," said Harrison, "sure it is." He fidgeted in his seat, feeling that he'd made a move and promptly lost a pawn. He sought around for something else to say and at that point a thin-featured man in a white coat dumped before him a large plate loaded with fried chicken and three kinds of unfamiliar food.

The sight unnerved him. He couldn't remember how many years it had been since he'd last seen fried chicken or how many months since he'd been offered vegetables in other than powder form.

"Well," demanded the waiter, mistaking his fascinated reaction, "doesn't it please you?"

"Yes." Harrison handed over the slip of paper. "Sure it does. You bet it does."

Glancing at the note, the other called to somebody semivisible at one end of the counter. "You've wiped out one of Jeff's." He strolled away, tearing the slip into small pieces.

"That was a fast pass," commented the brunette, nodding at the loaded plate. "He dumps a heavy feed-ob on you and you bounce it straight back, leaving all quits. I'll have to wash dishes to get rid of mine. Or kill one Seth has got on somebody else."

"I stacked a ton of canned stuff." Harrison picked up knife and fork, his mouth watering. There were no knives and forks on the ship; they weren't needed for powders and pills. "Don't give you much choice here, do they? You take what you get."

"Not if you've got an ob on Seth," she informed. "When you have, he must work it off the best way he can. You should have put that to him instead of waiting for fate and complaining afterward."

"But I'm not complaining."

"It's your right. That's freedom, isn't it?" She mused a bit, went on, "It isn't often I'm an ob ahead of Seth but when I am I scream for iced pineapple and he comes running. When *he's* one ahead *I* do the running." Her gray eyes narrowed in sudden suspicion. "You're listening as if all this is new to you. Are you a stranger here?"

He nodded, his mouth full of chicken. A little later he managed, "I'm off that spaceship."

"Good grief!" She froze considerably. "An Antigand! I wouldn't have thought it. Why, you look almost human."

"I've long taken pride in that similarity." He chewed, swallowed, looked inquiringly around. The white-coated man came up. "What's to drink?" Harrison asked.

"Dith, double-dith, shemak or coffee."

"Coffee. Big and black."

"Shemak is better," advised the brunette as the waiter went to get it. "But why should I tell you?"

The coffee came in a pint-sized mug. Putting it down, the waiter said, "It's your choice seeing that Seth is working one off. What'll you have for after—apple pie, yimpik delice, grated tarfelsoufers or canimelon in syrup?"

"Iced pineapple."

"Ugh!" The other blinked at him, gave the brunette an accusing stare, brought it and dumped it on the table.

Harrison pushed it across. "Take the plunge and enjoy yourself."

"It's yours."

"Couldn't eat it if I tried." He dug up another load of chicken, stirred his coffee, began to feel at perfect peace with this world. "Got as much as I can manage right here." He made an inviting motion with his fork. "Go on, be greedy and to heck with the waistline."

"No." Firmly she pushed the pineapple back at him. "If I ate my way through that I'd be saddled with an ob."

"So what?"

"I don't let strangers dump obs on me."

"Quite right, too. Very proper of you," approved Harrison. "Strangers often have strange notions."

"You've been around," she remarked. "Though I don't know what's strange about the notions."

"Cynic!" The pineapple got another pass in her direction. "If you feel that I'll be burdening you with an ob that you'll have to pay off you can do it in seemly manner here and now. All I want is some information."

"What is it?"

"Just tell me where I can put my finger on the ripest cheese in this locality."

"That's easy. Go round to Alec Peters' place, middle of Tenth Street." With that she helped herself to the dish.

"Thanks. I was beginning to think that everyone was dumb or afflicted with the funnies."

He carried on with his own meal, finished it, lay back expansively. Unaccustomed nourishment persuaded his brain to work a bit more dexterously and after a minute an expression of chronic doubt clouded his face and he inquired, "Does this Peters run a cheese warehouse?"

"Of course." Emitting a sigh of pleasure, she pushed the empty dish aside.

He groaned low down, then informed, "I'm chasing the mayor."

"What is that?"

"Number one. The big boss. The sheriff, pohanko, or whatever you call him."

"I'm still no wiser," she said, genuinely puzzled.

"The man who runs this town. The leading citizen."

"Make it a little clearer," she suggested, trying hard to help him. "Who or what should this citizen be leading?"

"You and Seth and everyone else." He waved a hand to encompass the entire burg.

Frowning, she asked, "Leading us *where?*"

"Wherever you're going."

She gave up, beaten, and signed the white-coated waiter to come to her assistance.

"Matt, are we going any place?"

"How should I know?"

"Well, ask Seth then."

He went away, came back with, "Seth says he's going home at six o'clock and what's it to you?"

"Anyone leading him there?" she inquired.

"Don't be daft," Matt advised. "He knows his own way and he's cold sober."

Harrison chipped in. "Look, I don't see why there should be so much difficulty about all this. Just tell me where I can find an official, any official—the police chief, the city treasurer, the mortuary keeper or even a mere justice of the peace."

"What's an official?" asked Matt, openly baffled.

"What's a justice of the peace?" added the brunette.

His mind side-slipped and did a couple of spins. It took him quite a time to reassemble his thoughts and try another tack.

"Let us suppose," he said to Matt, "that this joint catches fire. What would you do?"

"Fan it to keep it going," retorted Matt, fed up and making no effort to conceal the fact. He returned to the counter with the air of one not inclined to waste words on a congenial halfwit.

"He'd put it out," informed the brunette. "What else would you expect him to do?"

"Suppose that he couldn't?"

"He'd call in others to help him."

"And would they?"

"Of course." She surveyed him with a touch of pity. "They'd jump at the chance. They'd be planting a nice, big crop of strong obs, wouldn't they?"

"Yes, I guess so." He began to feel completely stalled but made a last desperate shot at the problem. "What if the fire were much too big and fast for passers-by to tackle?"

"Seth would summon the fire squad."

Defeat receded, triumph replaced it.

"Ah, so there is a fire squad? That's what I meant by something official. That's what I've been after all along. Quick, tell me where I can find its headquarters."

"Bottom end of Twelfth Avenue. You can't miss it."

"Thanks!" He got up in a hurry. "See you again sometime." Going out fast, he grabbed his bicycle, shoved off from the curb.

The fire depot proved to be a big place containing four telescopic ladders, a spray tower and two multiple pumps, all motorized on the usual array of fat rubber balls. Inside, Harrison came face to face with a small man wearing immense plus fours.

"Looking for someone?" asked the small man.

"Yes, the fire chief."

"Who's he?"

By now prepared for this sort of thing, Harrison spoke as one would to a child. "See here, Mister, this is a fire-fighting outfit. Somebody bosses it. Somebody organizes the whole affair, fills forms, presses buttons, shouts orders, recommends promotions, kicks the shiftless, grabs all the credit, transfers all the blame and generally lords it around. He's the most important man in the bunch and everybody knows it." His forefinger tapped imperatively on the other's chest. "And he is the fellow I'm going to talk to if it's the last thing I do."

"Nobody is more important than anyone else. How can he be? I think you're crazy."

"You're welcome to think what you please but I am telling you that——"

A shrill bell clamored, cutting off his sentence. Twenty men appeared as if by magic, boarded a ladder and a multiple pump, roared into the street.

Squat, basin-shaped helmets formed the only article of attire that the crew had in common. Apart from these, they plumbed the depths of sartorial iniquity. The man with the plus fours, having gained the pump in one bold leap, was whirled out standing between a fat fire-fighter wearing a rainbow-hued cummerbund and a thin one sporting a canary yellow kilt. A latecomer decorated with ear-rings resembling little bells hotly pursued the pump, snatched at its tailboard, missed, sourly watched the outfit disappear from sight. He mooched back, swinging his helmet from one hand.

"Just my lousy luck," he griped at the gaping Harrison. "The sweetest, loveliest call of the year. A big brewery. The sooner they get there the bigger the obs they'll plant on it." Licking his lips at the thought, he sat on a coil of canvas hose. "Oh, well, maybe it's for the good of my health."

"Tell me something," Harrison probed. "How do you make a living?"

"There's a dopey question. You can see for yourself. I'm on the fire squad."

"I know. What I mean is, who pays you?"

"Pays me?"

"Gives you money for all this."

"You talk mighty peculiar. What is money?"

Harrison rubbed his cranium to assist the circulation of blood through the brain. What is money? Yeouw! He tried another angle.

"If your wife needs a new coat, how does she get it?"

"Goes to a store that's carrying fire-obs, of course. She knocks off one or two for them."

"But what if no clothing store has had a fire?"

"You're pretty ignorant, brother. Where in this world do you come from?" His ear-bells swung as he studied the other a moment. "Almost all stores have fire-obs. If they've any sense they allocate so many per month by way of insurance. They look ahead, just in case, see? They plant obs on us in advance so that when we rush to the rescue we've got to wipe out a dollop of theirs before we can plant any new ones of our own. That stops us overdoing it and making hogs of ourselves. Sort of cuts down the stores' liabilities. It makes sense, doesn't it?"

"Maybe, but——"

"I get it now," interrupted the other, narrowing his eyes. "You're from that spaceship. You're a lousy Antigand."

"I'm a Terran," informed Harrison with suitable dignity. "What's more, all the folk who originally settled this planet were Terrans."

"Are you trying to teach me history?" He gave a harsh laugh. "You're wrong. There was a five percent strain of Martian."

"Even the Martians are descended from Terran stock," Harrison riposted.

"So what? That was a devil of a long time ago. Things change, in case you haven't heard. We've no Terrans or Martians on this world—except for your crowd which has barged in unasked. We've all Gands here. And you nosey-pokes are Antigands."

"We aren't anti-anything that I know of. Where did you get that idea?"

"Myob!" said the other, suddenly determined to refuse further argument. He tossed his helmet to one side, spat on the floor.

"Eh?"

"You heard me. Go trundle your scooter."

Harrison gave up and did just that. Gloomily he cycled back to the ship.

His Excellency pinned him with an authoritative optic. "So you're back at last, Mister. How many are coming and at what time?"

"None, sir," said Harrison, feeling kind of feeble.

"None?" August eyebrows lifted querulously. "Do you mean that they have refused my invitation?"

"No, sir."

"Come out with it, Mister," urged the Ambassador. "Don't stand there gawping as if your push-and-puff contraption has just given birth to a roller-skate. You say they have not refused my invitation—but nobody is coming. What am I supposed to make of that?"

"I didn't ask anyone."

"So you didn't ask?" Turning, he said to Grayder, Shelton and the others, "He didn't ask!" His attention came back to

Harrison. "You forgot all about it, I presume? Intoxicated by liberty and the power of man over machine, you flashed around the town at nothing less than eighteen miles per hour, creating consternation among the citizenry, tossing their traffic laws into the ash-can, putting children and elderly persons in peril of their lives, not even troubling to ring your bell or——"

"I don't have a bell, sir," stated Harrison, inwardly resenting this list of enormities. "I have a whistle operated by the rotation of the rear wheel."

"There!" said the Ambassador like one abandoning all hope. He sat down and smacked his forehead several times. "I am reliably informed that somebody is going to get a bubble-pipe." He pointed at Harrison. "And now I learn that *he* possesses a whistle."

"I designed it myself, sir," Harrison said helpfully.

"I'm sure you did. I can imagine it. I would expect it of you." The Ambassador took a fresh grip on himself. "See here, Mister, I would like you to tell me something in strict confidence, just between the two of us." Leaning forward, he put the question in a whisper that ricochetted seven times around the room. "*Why* didn't you ask anyone?"

"I couldn't find out who to ask, sir. I did my level best but nobody seemed to know what I was talking about. Or they pretended they didn't."

"Humph!" The Ambassador glanced out of the nearest port, consulted his watch. "The light is fading already. Night will be upon us pretty soon. It's too late for further action." An annoyed grunt. "Another day gone to pot. Two days here and we're still fiddling around." Then he added with grim resignation, "All right, Mister. We're wasting time anyway so we might as well hear your story in full. Tell us what happened in complete detail. That way, we may be able to dig some sense out of it."

Harrison told it, finishing, "It seemed to me, sir, that I could carry on for weeks trying to argue it out with people whose brains are oriented east-west while mine point north-south. One can talk with them from now to doomsday, become really friendly and enjoy the conversation—without either side fully understanding what the other is saying."

"So it appears," said the Ambassador dryly. He turned to Grayder. "You've been around a lot and seen many new worlds in your time. What do you make of all this twaddle, if anything?"

"It's a problem in semantics," diagnosed Grayder, who had been compelled by circumstances to study that subject. "One comes across it on many worlds that have been long out of touch, though usually it hasn't developed far enough to become tough and unsolvable. For instance, the first fellow we met on Basileus said, cordially and in what he imagined to be perfect Terran, 'Joy you unboot now!'"

"Yes? And what did that mean?"

"Come inside, put on your slippers and be happy. In other words, welcome. It wasn't difficult to understand, Your Excellency, especially when one expects that sort of thing." Grayder cast a thoughtful glance at Harrison and continued, "Here, the problem seems to have developed to a greater extreme. The language remains fluent and retains enough surface similarities to conceal underlying changes, but basic meanings have been altered, concepts discarded and new ones substituted, thought-forms re-angled and, of course, there is the inevitable impact of locally created slang."

"Such as 'Myob,'" offered the Ambassador. "Now there is a queer word without recognizable Earth-root. I don't like the sarcastic way they use it. They make it sound downright insulting. Obviously it has some kind of connection with these obs they keep throwing around. It means 'my obligation' or something like that, but the real significance eludes me."

"There is no connection, sir," put in Harrison. He hesitated, saw that they were waiting for him to go on. "On my way back I met the lady who had directed me to Baines' place. She asked whether I'd found him and I told her I had. We chatted a short while. I asked her what 'Myob' meant. She said it was initial-slang."

"Keep going," urged the Ambassador. "After some of the sulphurous comments I've heard emerging from the Blieder-room ventilation-shaft, I can stomach anything. What does it mean?"

"M-y-o-b," informed Harrison, slightly embarrassed. "Mind-your-own-business."

"Ah!" The other gained color. "So *that* is what they've been telling me all along?"

"I'm afraid so, sir."

"Evidently they've a lot to learn." His neck swelled with undiplomatic fury, he smacked a fat hand upon the table and declaimed loudly, "And they're going to learn it!"

"Yes, sir," agreed Harrison, becoming more uneasy and anxious to get out. "May I go now and tend to my bicycle?"

"Yes, you may," said the Ambassador in the same noisy

tones. He performed a couple of meaningless gestures, turned a florid face on Captain Grayder. "Bicycle! Does anyone on this vessel own a sling-shot?"

"I doubt it, Your Excellency, but I will make inquiries, if you wish."

"Don't be an imbecile," ordered the Ambassador. "We have our full quota of hollow-heads already."

10

Postponed until early morning, the next conference was relatively short and sweet. The Ambassador took a seat, harumphed importantly, straightened his tie, frowned around the table.

"Let us have another look at what we've got. We know that this planet's mules call themselves Gands, don't take any interest in their Terran origin and insist on referring to us as Antigands. This implies an education and resultant outlook inimical to ourselves. They've been trained from childhood to take it for granted that whenever we appeared upon the scene we would prove to be against whatever they are for."

"And we haven't the remotest notion of what they are for," put in Colonel Shelton, quite unnecessarily. But it served to show that he was among those present, paying full attention, and ready to lend the full support of his powerful intellect.

"I am only too aware of our ignorance in that respect," said the Ambassador, with a touch of acid. "They are maintaining a conspiracy of silence about their prime motivation. We have got to break it somehow."

"That," offered Shelton, unabashed, "is the problem."

Taking no notice, the Ambassador continued, "They have a peculiar, moneyless economic system which, in my opinion, manages to function only because it is afflicted with large surpluses. It won't survive a day when over-population brings serious shortages. This economic set-up appears to be based on a mixture of coöperative techniques, private enterprise, a kindergarten's honor system and plain, unadorned gimme. That makes it a good deal crazier than the food-in-the-bank system they use on Epsilon's four outer planets."

"But it works," observed Grayder pointedly.

"After a fashion. That flap-eared engineer's bicycle works—

and so does he while riding it. A motorized job would save him a lot of sweat." Highly pleased with this analogy, the Ambassador enjoyed the flavor of it for a few seconds before he continued. "This local scheme of economics—if you can call it a scheme—almost certainly is the end-result of the haphazard development of some hick eccentricity imported by the original settlers. It is long overdue for motorizing, so to speak. They know it as well as we do. But they don't want it because mentally they're four hundred years behind the times. They are afraid of change, improvement, efficiency— like many backward peoples. Moreover, there's little doubt that some of them have a vested interest in keeping things exactly as they are." He sniffed loudly to express his contempt. "They are antagonistic toward us simply because they don't want to be disturbed."

His stare went round the table, daring one of them to remark that this might be as good a reason as any other. They were too disciplined to fall into that trap. None offered a comment and so he went on.

"In due time, after we have gained a proper grip on affairs, we're going to have a long and tedious task on our hands. We'll have to overhaul their entire educational system with a view to eliminating anti-Terran prejudices and bringing them up to date on the facts of life. That's had to be done on several other planets though not to anything like the extent as will be necessary here."

"We'll cope," promised someone.

Ignoring him, the Ambassador finished, "However, all that is in the future. Our real problem is in the present. It is in our laps right now, namely, where are the reins of power and who is holding them? We must solve that before we can make genuine progress. How are we going to do it?" Folding hands over his paunch, he added, "Get your wits to work and let us have some bright suggestions."

Grayder stood up, a big, leather-bound book in his hands. "Your Excellency, I don't think we need exercise our minds about new plans for making contact and gaining essential information. The next move is likely to be imposed upon us."

"What do you mean?"

"I have a good many old-timers in my crew. There are some among the troops as well. Space-lawyers, every one of them." He tapped the book significantly. "They know Space Regulations as well as I do. Sometimes I think they know too much."

"And so——?"

Grayder opened the book. "Regulation 127 says that on

a hostile world the crew serves on a war-footing until back in free space. On a non-hostile world they serve on a peace-footing."

"What of it?"

"Regulation 131A says that on a peace-footing the crew—with the exception of a minimum number required to keep the vessel's services in trim—is entitled to liberty immediately after unloading cargo or within seventy-two Earth-hours of arrival, whichever period is the shorter." He glanced up. "By mid-day the men will be all set for land-leave and itching to go. There will be trouble if they are not allowed out."

"Oh, will there?" The Ambassador smiled lopsidedly. "What if we declare this world to be hostile? That will pin their ears back, won't it?"

Impassively consulting his book, Grayder said, "Regulation 148 says that a hostile world is defined as any planet that systematically opposes Terran citizens by force." He turned to the next page. "For the purpose of these regulations, force is defined as any course of action calculated to inflict physical injury, regardless of whether or not the said action succeeds in its intent."

"I don't agree." The Ambassador frowned his strong disapproval. "A world can be psychologically hostile without resorting to force. We have an example right here. It can't be called a friendly world."

"There are no friendly worlds within the meaning of Space Regulations," Grayder informed. "Every planet falls into one of two classifications: hostile or non-hostile." He tapped the hard leather cover. "It's all in the book."

"We'd be prize fools to let a mere book order us around or allow the crew to boss us, either. Throw it out of the port. Stick it into the disintegrator. Get rid of it any way you like—and forget it."

"Begging your pardon, Your Excellency, but I can't do that." Grayder opened the tome at its beginning. "Basic regulations 1A, 1B and 1C include the following: whether in space or on land, a vessel's personnel remain under direct command of its captain or his nominee who will be guided solely and at all times by Space Regulations and will be responsible only to the Space Committee situated on Terra. The same applies to all troops, officials and civilian passengers aboard a space-traversing vessel, whether said vessel is in flight or grounded—regardless of rank or authority they are subordinate to the captain or his nominee. A nominee is defined as a ship's first, second or third officer performing the duties of a captain when the latter is incapacitated or absent."

"What all that rigmarole means is that you are king of your castle," remarked the Ambassador, none too pleased. "If we don't like it we must get out of the ship."

"With the greatest respect, Your Excellency, I must agree that that is the position. I cannot help it—regulations are regulations. And the men know it!" Grayder placed the book on the table, poked it away from him. "It's highly likely that the men will wait until mid-day, pressing their pants, creaming their hair and generally prettying themselves up. They will then make approach to me in proper manner to which I cannot object. They will request the first mate to submit their leave roster for my approval." He gave a deep sigh. "The worst I could do would be to quibble about a few names and switch some of them around. But I cannot refuse leave to a full quota."

"Liberty to paint the town red might be a good thing after all," suggested Shelton, not averse to doing some painting himself. "A dump like this wakes up with a vengeance when the fleet's in port. We should make useful contacts by the dozens. And that's what we want, isn't it?"

"We want to pin down this planet's political leaders," retorted the Ambassador. "I can't see them powdering their faces, putting on their best hats and rushing out to give the yoohoo to a crowd of hungry sailors." His plump features quirked. "We've got to find the needles in this haystack and that job won't be done by ratings on the rampage."

"You may be right, Your Excellency," put in Grayder. "But we'll have to take a chance on it. If the men insist on going out I lack the power to prevent them. Only one thing can give me the power."

"And what is that?"

"Clear, indisputable evidence enabling me to define this world as hostile within the meaning of Space Regulations."

"Well, can't we arrange that somehow?" Without waiting for a reply, the Ambassador pursued, "Every crew has its stupid and incurable trouble-maker. Find yours, give him a double shot of Venusian cognac, tell him he's being granted immediate liberty—then warn him that he may not enjoy it because these lousy Gands view us as a reason why people dig up the drains. After that, push him out of the airlock. When he returns with a black eye and a boastful story about the other fellow's condition, declare this world hostile." He waved an expressive hand. "And there you are. Physical violence. All according to the book."

"Regulation 148A," said Grayder, "emphasizing that opposition by force must be systematic, warns that individual brawls may not be construed as evidence of hostility."

The Ambassador turned an irate face upon the senior civil servant. "When you return to Terra—if ever you do get back—you can tell the appropriate department how the space service is balled up, hamstrung, semi-paralysed and generally handicapped by bureaucrats who write books."

Before the other could think up a reply in defence of his own kind, without contradicting the Ambassador, a knock came at the door. First Mate Morgan entered, saluted smartly, offered Grayder a sheet of paper.

"First leave roster, sir. Do you approve it?"

More than four hundred men went to town in the early afternoon. They advanced upon it in the usual manner of people long overdue for the bright lights, that is to say, eagerly, expectantly, in gangs of two, three, six or ten.

Gleed attached himself to Harrison. They were two odd rankers, Gleed being the only sergeant on liberty while Harrison was the only tenth engineer. They were also the only two fish out of water since both were in civilian clothes and Gleed missed his uniform, Harrison felt naked without his bicycle. These trifling features gave them enough in common to justify at least one day's companionship.

"This one's a honey," declared Gleed with great enthusiasm. "I've been on a good many liberty jaunts in my time but this one's a honey. On all other trips the boys ran up against the same problem: what to use for money. They had to go forth like a battalion of Santa Clauses, loaded up with anything that might serve for barter. Almost always nine-tenths of it wasn't of any use and had to be carted back to the ship."

"On Persephone," informed Harrison, "a long-shanked Milik offered me a twenty-karat, blue-tinted, first-water diamond for my bike."

"Jeepers, didn't you take it?"

"What was the good? I'd have had to go back sixteen light-years for another bike."

"But, man, you could exist without a bike for a while."

"I can exist without a diamond. I can't ride around on a diamond."

"Neither can you sell a bicycle for the price of a sportster Moon-boat."

"Yes, I can. I just told you this Milik offered me a rock like an egg."

"It's a crying shame. You could have got a fortune for that blinder, if it had no flaws." Sergeant Gleed smacked his lips at the thought of it. "Money and plenty of it, that's what I like. And that's what makes this trip a winner. Every other time we've gone out, Grayder, Shelton and Bidworthy have lectured us in turn about creating a favorable impression, behaving in a spacemanlike manner and so forth. But this time Grayder talks about money."

"The Ambassador put him up to it."

"I like it all the same," enthused Gleed. "An extra one week's pay, a bottle of cognac and double liberty for any man who brings back to the ship an adult Gand, male or female, who is sociable and willing to talk."

"It won't be easily earned."

"One month's extra pay for whoever gets the name and address of the town's chief civic dignitary. Two months' for the name and accurate location of the world's capital city." He whistled happily, added, "Somebody is going to make it rich and it won't be Bidworthy. His name didn't come out of the hat. I know—I was holding it."

Ceasing his chatter, he turned to watch a tall, lithe blonde striding past. Harrison pulled at his arm.

"Here's Baines' place that I told you about. Let's go in."

"Oh, all right." Gleed followed with reluctance, his attention still directed down the street.

"Good afternoon," said Harrison to Jeff Baines.

"Which it isn't," contradicted Baines. "Trade's bad. There's a semi-final being played and it has drawn half the town away. They'll come home and start thinking about their bellies long after I've closed. Probably they'll make a rush on me tomorrow morning and I won't be able to serve them fast enough."

"How can trade be bad if you don't make money even when it's good?" inquired Gleed, reasonably applying the information Harrison had given him.

Jeff's big moon eyes went over him slowly then turned to Harrison. "So he's another bum off your boat, eh? What's he talking about?"

"Money," explained Harrison. "It's stuff we use to simplify trade. It's printed stuff, like documentary obs of various sizes."

"That tells me a lot," Jeff Baines observed. "It tells a crowd that has to make a printed record of every ob is not to

e trusted—because they don't even trust each other." He
addled to his high stool and squated on it. His breathing was
bored and wheezy. "And that confirms what our schools have
ways taught, namely, that an Antigand would swindle his
idowed mother."

"Your schools have got it wrong," assured Harrison.

"Maybe they have." Jeff saw no reason to argue the point.
But we'll play safe until we know different." He looked
em over. "What do you two want, anyway?"

"Some advice," Gleed shoved in quickly. "We're out on the
ree. We'd like to know the best places for food and fun."

"How long have you got?"

"Until nightfall tomorrow."

"No use." Jeff Baines shook his head sorrowfully. "It would
ke you from now until then to plant enough obs to qualify
r anything worth having. Besides, plenty of people would
ther drop dead than let an Antigand dump an ob on them.
hey have their pride, see?"

Harrison asked, "Can't we get so much as a square meal?"

"Well, I don't know about that." Jeff thought it over while
assaging his several chins. "You might manage it—but I
n't help you this time. There's nothing I want of you and
you can't use any obs I've got stashed around."

"Can you offer any suggestions?"

"If you were local citizens it would be lots different. You
uld get all you want right now by taking on a load of obs
be wiped out sometime in the future as and when the
ances come along. But I can't see anybody giving credit
Antigands who are here today and gone tomorrow."

"Not so much of the gone tomorrow talk," advised Gleed.
When an Imperial Ambassador arrives it means that Terrans
e here for keeps."

"Who says so?"

"The Terran Empire says so. You're part of it, aren't you?"

"No," said Jeff positively. "We are not part of anything,
n't want to be and don't intend to be. What's more,
body's going to make us part of anything."

Leaning on the counter, Gleed gazed absently at a large
n of pork. "Seeing that I'm out of uniform and not on duty,
sympathize with you though I still shouldn't say it. I
ouldn't care myself to be taken over body and soul by a
ang of other-world bureaucrats. But you folk are going to
ave a mighty tough time beating us off. That's the way it is."

"Not with what we've got," opined Jeff confidently.

"You haven't got much," scoffed Gleed, more in friendly

criticism than open contempt. He sought confirmation from Harrison. "Have they?"

"It wouldn't seem so," said Harrison.

"Don't go by appearances," warned Jeff. "We've more than you bums can handle."

"Such as what?"

"Well, just for a start, we've got the mightiest weapon ever thought up by the mind of man. We're Gands, see? So we don't need ships and guns and similar playthings. We've something better. It's effective. There's no defence against it."

"Man, I'd like to see it," Gleed challenged. Data concerning a new and exceptionally powerful weapon should be a good deal more valuable than the mayor's address. Grayder might be sufficiently impressed by the importance thereof to arrange a fabulous reward. With some sarcasm, he added, "But, of course, we can't expect you to give away precious secrets."

"There is nothing secret about it," said Jeff, very surprisingly. "You can have it free, gratis and for nothing any time you want. And Gand would give it to you for the mere asking. Like to know why?"

"You bet."

"Because it works one way only. We can use it against you—but you can't use it against us."

"Nonsense!" declared Gleed. "There is no such thing. There is no weapon inventable that the other fellow can't employ once he gets his hands on it and learns how to operate it."

"Are you sure about that?"

"I am positive. I've been in the space service for twenty years. You can't be a trooper that long without learning all about weapons of every conceivable kind from string bows to H-bombs. You're trying to kid me. Nothing doing. I'm too gray in the hair and sharp in the tooth. A one-way weapon is impossible. And that means *im-poss-ible.*"

"Don't argue with him," Harrison told Baines. "He'll never be convinced until he's shown."

"I can see that." Jeff Baines' face creased into a massive grin. "I've told you that you can have our wonder-weapon for the asking. Why don't you ask?"

"All right, I'm asking." Gleed put it without any enthusiasm. A weapon that would be presented on request, without even the necessity of first planting a minor ob, couldn't be so mighty after all. His imaginary large reward shrank to a handful of small change and thence to nothing. "Hand over and let me look at it."

Edging ponderously around on his stool, Jeff reached to the wall, removed a small, shiny plaque from its hook and passed it across the counter.

"You may keep it," he said. "And much good may it do you."

Gleed examined it, turning it over and over between his fingers. It was nothing more than an oblong strip of substance resembling ivory. One side was polished and bare. The other bore three letters deeply engraved in bold style:

F.—I.W.

Glancing up at Baines, his features puzzled, he said, "You call this a weapon?"

"Certainly."

"Then I don't get it." He passed the plaque to Harrison. "Do you?"

"No." Harrison examined it with care. "What does this F.—I.W. mean?"

"Initial-slang," informed Baines. "Made còrrect by common usage. It has become a worldwide motto. You'll see it all over the place if you haven't noticed it already."

"I have seen it here and there but attached no importance to it and thought nothing more about it. I remember now that it was inscribed in several places including Seth's and the fire depot."

"It was on the sides of that bus we couldn't empty," put in Gleed. "It didn't mean anything to me."

"It means plenty," said Jeff. "*Freedom—I Won't!*"

"That kills me," Gleed responded. "I'm stone dead already. I've dropped in my tracks." He watched Harrison thoughtfully pocketing the plaque. "A piece of abracadabre. What a weapon!"

"Ignorance is bliss," asserted Baines, strangely sure of himself. "Especially when you don't know that what you're playing with is the safety catch of something that goes bang."

"All right," challenged Gleed, taking him up on that. "Tell us how it works."

"I won't." Baines' grin reappeared. He seemed to be highly satisfied about something.

"That's a fat lot of help." Gleed felt let down, especially over that momentary hoped-for reward. "You brag and boast about a one-way weapon, toss across a slip of stuff with three letters on it and then go dumb. Any folly will do for braggarts and any braggart can talk through the seat of his pants. How about backing up your talk?"

"I won't," repeated Baines, his grin broader than ever. He gave the onlooking Harrison a fat, significant wink.

It made something spark vividly within Harrison's mind. His jaw dropped, he dragged the plaque from his pocket and stared at it as if seeing it for the first time.

"Give it back to me," requested Baines, watching him.

Replacing it in his pocket, Harrison said very firmly, "I won't."

Baines chuckled. "Some people catch on quicker than others."

Resenting that, Gleed held his hand out to Harrison. "Let me have another look at that thing."

"I won't," said Harrison, meeting him eye to eye.

"Hey, don't start being awkward with me. That's not the way——" Gleed's protesting voice petered out. He stood there a moment, his optics slightly glassy, while his brain performed several loops. Then in hushed tones he said, "Good grief!"

"Precisely," approved Baines. "Grief and plenty of it. You were a bit slow on the uptake."

Overcome by the flood of insubordinate ideas now pouring upon him, Gleed said hoarsely to Harrison, "Come on, let's get out of here. I've got to think. I want to sit somewhere nice and quiet while I think."

There was a tiny park with seats and lawns and flowers and a little fountain around which a small group of children were playing. Choosing a place facing a colorful carpet of exotic un-Terran blooms, they sat and brooded for quite a time.

Eventually, Gleed commented, "For one solitary, mulish character it would be martydrom, but for a whole world——" His voice drifted off, came back. "I've been taking this as far as I can make it go and the results give me the leaping fantods."

Harrison said nothing.

"For instance," Gleed continued. "Suppose that when I go back to the ship that snorting rhinoceros Bidworthy gives me an order. And I give him the frozen eye and say, 'I won't.' What happens? It follows as an inviolable law of Nature that he either drops dead or throws me in the clink."

"That would do you a lot of good."

"Wait a bit—I haven't finished yet. I'm in the pokey, demoted and a disgrace to the service, but the job still needs doing. So Bidworthy picks on somebody else. The victim, being a soul-mate of mine, also donates the icy optic and says, 'I won't.' Into the jug he goes and I've got company.

Bidworthy tries again. And again and again and again. There are more of us crammed in the brig. It will hold only twenty. So they take over the engineers' mess."

"Leave our mess out of this," requested Harrison.

"They take over the mess," insisted Gleed, thoroughly determined to penalize the engineers. "Pretty soon it's filled to the roof with I-won'ters. Bidworthy is still raking them in as fast as he can go—if by then he hasn't burst a dozen blood vessels. So they take over the Blieder dormitories."

"Why keep picking on my crowd?"

"And pile them ceiling-high with bodies," Gleed said, deriving sadistic pleasure from the picture. "Until in the end Bidworthy has to get buckets and brushes and go down on his knees and do his own deck-scrubbing while Grayder, Shelton and the rest take turn for guard-duty. By that time His Loftiness the Ambassador is in the galley busily cooking for the prisoners and is being assisted by a disconcerted bunch of yessing pen-pushers." He had another look at this mental scene. "Holy smoke!"

A colored ball rolled his way. Stooping, he picked it up, held on to it. Promptly a boy of about seven ran near, eyed him gravely.

"Give me my ball, please."

"I won't" said Gleed, his fingers firmly around it.

There were no protest, no anger, no tears. The child merely registered disappointment and turned away.

"Here you are, sonny." He tossed the ball.

"Thanks." Grabbing it, the other chased off.

Harrison said, "What if every living being in the Terran Empire, from Prometheus to Kaldor Four, across eighteen hundred light-years of space, should get an income-tax demand, tear it up and say, 'I won't.' What happens then?"

"No tax. Authority does without it because it darned well has to."

"There would be chaos." Harrison nodded toward the fountain and the children playing around it. "But it doesn't look anything like chaos here. Not to my eyes. Evidently they don't overdo this blank refusal business. They apply it judiciously on some mutually recognized basis. But what that basis might be beats me completely."

"Me, too."

An elderly man paused near them, surveyed them hesitantly, decided to pick on a passing youth.

"Can you tell me where I can find the roller for Martinstown?"

"Other end of Eighth," directed the youth. "One every hour. They'll fix your manacles before they start."

"Manacles?" The oldster raised white eyebrows. "Whatever for?"

"That route runs past the spaceship. The Antigands may try to drag you out."

"Oh, yes, of course." He ambled on, glanced again at Gleed and Harrison, remarked in passing, "These Antigands—such a nuisance."

"Definitely," supported Gleed. "We keep telling them to clear out and they keep saying, 'We won't.'"

The old gentleman missed a step, recovered, gave him a peculiar look, continued on his way.

"One or two seem to cotton on to our accent," Harrison said. "Though nobody baulked at mine when I was having that meal in Seth's."

Gleed perked up with sudden interest. "Where you've had one feed you should be able to get another. Come on, let's try. What have we to lose?"

"Our patience." Harrison got off his seat, stretched himself. "We'll pick on Seth. If he won't play we'll have a try at somebody else. And if nobody will play we'll scoot back to the ship before we starve to death."

"Which appears to be exactly what they want us to do," Gleed pointed out with some annoyance. "I can tell you something here and now—they'll get their way over my dead body."

"That's how," agreed Harrison. "Over your dead body."

11

Matt came up with a cloth over one arm. "I'm serving no Antigands."

"You served me last time," Harrison reminded.

"That may be. I didn't know you were off that ship. But I know now." He flicked the cloth across one corner of the table, brushing away imaginary crumbs. "No Antigands served by me."

"Is there any other place where we might get a meal?"

"Not unless somebody will let you plant an ob on them. They won't do that if they know who you are but there's a chance they might make the same mistake as I did." Another flick across the corner. "I don't make them twice."

"You're making one right now," announced Gleed, his voice hard and edgy. He nudged Harrison. "Watch this." His hand came out of a side pocket holding a tiny gun. Pointing it at Matt's middle, he said, "Ordinarily I could get into trouble for this, if those on the ship were in the mood to make trouble. But they aren't. They're more than tired of you two-legged mules." He motioned with the weapon. "So start walking and fetch us two full plates."

"I won't," said Matt, firming his lips and ignoring the gun.

Gleed thumbed the safety-catch which moved with an audible click. "It's touchy now. It'd go off at a sneeze. Get moving."

"I won't," said Matt.

With unconcealed disgust, Gleed shoved the weapon back into his pocket. "I was only kidding you. It isn't loaded."

"Wouldn't have made the slightest difference if it had been," Matt assured. "I serve no Antigands and that is that."

"What if I'd lost control of myself and blown several large holes in you?"

"How could I have served you then?" asked Matt. "A dead person is of no use to anyone. It's time you Antigands learned a little logic." With which parting shot he meandered off.

"He's got something there," offered Harrison, patently depressed. "What can you do with a corpse? Nothing whatever. A body is in nobody's power."

"Oh, I don't know. A couple of stiffs lying around might sharpen the others. They'd become really eager."

"You're thinking of them in Terran terms," Harrison said. "It's a mistake. They are not Terrans no matter where they came from originally. They are Gands."

"Well, just what are Gands supposed to be?"

"I don't know. It's a safe bet they're some kind of fanatics. Terra exported one-track-minders by the millions around the time of the Great Explosion. Look at that crazy crowd on Hygeia, for instance."

"Ah, Hygeia. That was the only time I've ever strutted around wearing nothing but a dignified pose. I was looking forward to seeing Shelton and Bidworthy in their birthday suits. But those two heroes both lacked the guts." He chuckled to himself, went on, "Those Hygeians think that complete nakedness creates real democracy, as distinct from our fake version. I'm far from sure that they're wrong."

"The creation of an empire has also created a cockeyed

proposition," mediated Harrison. "Namely, that Terra is always right while more than sixteen hundred planets are invariably wrong. Everyone is out of step but Terra."

"You're becoming kind of seditious, aren't you?"

Harrison offered no reply. Gleed glanced at him, found his attention diverted elsewhere, followed his gaze to a brunette who had just entered.

"Nice," approved Gleed. "Not too old, not too young. Not too fat, not too thin. Just right."

"I know her." Harrison waved to attract her attention.

She tripped lightly across the room, took a chair at their table. Harrison made the introduction.

"Friend of mine, Sergeant Gleed."

"Arthur," corrected Gleed, guzzling her with his eyes.

"Mine's Elissa," she told him. "What's a sergeant supposed to be?"

"A sort of over-above under-thing," said Gleed. "I pass along the telling to the fellows who do the doing."

She viewed him with frank surprise. "Do you mean that people actually allow themselves to be *told?*"

"Of course. Why not?"

"They must have been born servile." Her gaze shifted to Harrison. "I'll be ignorant of your name forever, I suppose?"

Flushing slightly, he hastened to repair the omission, adding, "But I don't like James. I prefer Jim."

"Then we'll let it be Jim. Has Matt tended to you two yet?"

"He refuses to serve us."

She shrugged soft, warm shoulders. "It's his right. That's freedom, isn't it?"

"We call it mutiny," said Gleed.

"Don't be childish," she reproved. She stood up, moved away. "You wait here. I'll see what Seth says."

"I don't understand this," admitted Gleed when she had passed out of earshot. "According to that fat fellow in the delicatessen, their technique is to give us the cold shoulder until we run away in a huff. But she's . . . she's——" He stopped while he sought around for a suitable word, found it and said, "She's un-Gandian."

"Not so," Harrison contradicted. "They've the right to say, 'I won't' any way they like. She's practicing it."

"By gosh, yes. I hadn't thought of that. They can work it backward or forward, whichever way they please."

"That's right." Harrison lowered his voice. "Here she comes."

Resuming her seat, she primped her hair and said, "Seth will serve us personally."

"Another traitor," remarked Gleed, grinning.

"On one condition," she went on. "You two must wait and have a talk with him before you leave."

"It's cheap at the price," Harrison decided. Another thought struck him. "Does this mean you'll have to wipe out several obs for all three of us?"

"Only one for myself."

"How's that?"

"Seth's got ideas of his own. He doesn't feel happy about Antigands any more than anyone else does."

"And so——?"

"But he has the missionary instinct. He doesn't agree entirely with the habit of giving all Antigands the ghost-treatment. He thinks it should be reserved only for those too stubborn or stupid to be converted." She smiled at Gleed, making his top hairs quiver. "Seth thinks that any really intelligent Antigand is a would-be Gand."

"What is a Gand, anyway?" asked Harrison.

"An inhabitant of this world, of course."

"I mean how did they get that name? From where did they dig it up?"

"From Gandhi," she said.

Harrison looked blank. "Who the deuce was he?"

"An ancient Terran. The one who invented The Weapon."

"Never heard of him."

"That doesn't surprise me," she remarked.

"Doesn't it?" He was irritated by this confidence in his ignorance. "Let me tell you that in these days we Terrans get as good an education as——"

"Calm down, Jim," she advised, making it more soothing by pronouncing it, "Jeem." She patted his arm. "What I mean is that it's highly likely that he's blanked out of your history books. He might have given you unwanted ideas, see? You couldn't be expected to know what you've never been given the chance to learn."

"If you're saying that Terran history is censored, I don't believe it."

"It's your right to refuse to believe. That's freedom, isn't it?"

"Up to a point."

"To what point?"

"A man has duties. He has no right to refuse those."

"No?" She raised tantalizing eyebrows, delicately curved. "Who defines those duties—himself or somebody else?"

"His superiors most times."

"Superiors," she scoffed with devastating scorn. "No man is superior to another. No man has the slightest right to define another man's duties. If anyone on Terra exercises such impudent power it is only because idiots permit him to do so. They fear freedom. They prefer to be told. They like to be ordered around. They love their chains and kiss their manacles. What men!"

"I shouldn't listen to you," protested Gleed, chipping in. His leathery face was flushed. "You're almost as naughty as you're pretty."

"Afraid of your own thoughts?" she jibed, ignoring his lop-sided compliment.

He went redder. "Not on your life. But I——" His voice tailed off as Seth arrived with three loaded plates and dumped them on the table.

"See you afterward," reminded Seth. He was medium-sized, with thin features and sharp, quick-moving eyes. "Got something to say to you."

Seth joined them shortly after they'd finished their meal. Taking a chair, he wiped condensed steam off his face, looked them over calculatingly.

"How much do you two know?"

"Enough to fight over it," put in Elissa. "They are bothered about duties, who defines them and who performs them."

"With good reason," Harrison counter-attacked. "You can't escape them yourselves."

"Is that so?" said Seth. "How d'you make that out?"

"This world runs on some strange system of swapping obligations. How would any person cancel an ob unless he recognized it as his duty to do so?"

"Duty nothing," declared Seth. "Duty hasn't anything to do with it. And if it did happen to be a matter of duty every man would be left to recognize it for himself. It would be outrageous impertinence for anyone to remind him, unthinkable that anyone should order him."

"Some guys must make an easy living," interjected Gleed. "There's nothing to stop that that I can see." He studied Seth briefly before he asked, "How can you cope with a citizen who has no conscience?"

Elissa suggested, "Tell them the story of Idle Jack."

"It's a kids' yarn," explained Seth. "All children here know it by heart. It's a classic fable like . . . like——" He screwed up his face. "I've lost track of the Terran tales the first-comers brought with them."

"Red Riding Hood," offered Harrison.

"Yes." Seth seized upon it gratefully. "Something like that one. A nursery story." He licked his lips, began, "This Idle Jack came from Terra as a baby, grew up in our new world, gained an understanding of our economic system and thought he'd be mighty smart. He decided to become a scratcher."

"What's a scratcher?" asked Gleed.

"One who lives by accepting obs but does nothing about wiping them out or planting any of his own. One who takes everything that's going and gives nothing in return."

"We've still got 'em," said Gleed.

"Up to age sixteen Jack got away with it all along the line. He was only a kid, see? All kids tend to scratch to a certain extent. We expect it and allow for it. But after sixteen he was soon in the soup."

"How?" urged Harrison, more interested than he was willing to admit.

"He loafed around the town gathering obs by the armful. Meals, clothes and all sorts for the mere asking. It wasn't a big town. There are no big ones on this planet. They are just small enough for everybody to know everybody—and everyone does plenty of gabbing. Within a few months the entire town knew that Jack was a determined and incorrigible scratcher."

"Go on," said Harrison impatiently.

"Everything dried up," responded Seth. "Wherever Jack went people gave him the, 'I won't.' He got no meals, no clothes, no company, no entertainment, nothing. He was avoided like a leper. Soon he became terribly hungry, busted into someone's larder one night, treated himself to the first square meal in a week."

"What did they do about that?"

"Nothing, not a thing."

"That must have encouraged him some, mustn't it?"

"How could it?" asked Seth with a thin smile. "It did him no good. Next day his belly was empty again. He was forced to repeat the performance. And the next day. And the next. People then became leery, locked up their stuff and kept watch on it. Circumstances grew harder and harder. They grew so unbearably hard that soon it was a lot easier to leave the town and try another one. So Idle Jack went away."

"To do the same again," Harrison prompted.

"With the same results for the same reasons," Seth threw back at him. "On he went to a third town, a fourth, a fifth, a twentieth. He was stubborn enough to be witless."

"But he was getting by," Harrison insisted. "Taking all for nothing at the cost of moving around."

"Oh, no he wasn't. Our towns are small, as I said. And people do plenty of visiting from one to another. In the second town Jack had to risk being seen and talked about by visitors from the first town. In the third town he had to cope with talkers from both the first and second ones. As he went on it became a whole lot worse. In the twentieth he had to chance being condemned by anyone coming from any of the previous nineteen." Seth leaned forward, said with emphasis, "He never reached town number twenty-eight."

"No?"

"He lasted two weeks in number twenty-five, eight days in number twenty-six, one day in twenty-seven. That was almost the end. He knew he's be recognized the moment he showed his face in number twenty-eight."

"What did he do then?"

"He took to the open country, tried to live like an animal feeding on roots and wild berries. Then he disappeared—until one day some walkers found him swinging from a tree. His body was emaciated and clad in rags. Loneliness, self-neglect and his own stupidity had combined to kill him. That was Idle Jack, the scratcher. He wasn't twenty years old."

"On Terra," remarked Gleed virtuously, "we don't hang people merely for being shiftless and lazy."

"Neither de we," said Seth. "We give them every encouragement to go hang themselves. And when they do it's good riddance to bad rubbish." He eyed them shrewdly as he went on, "But don't let it worry you. Nobody has been driven to such drastic measures in my lifetime, leastways, not that I've heard about. People honor their obs as a matter of economic necessity and not from any sense of duty. Nobody gives orders, nobody pushes anyone around, but there's a kind of compulsion built into the circumstances of this planet's way of life. People play square—or they suffer. Nobody enjoys suffering, not even a numbskull."

"Yes, I suppose you're right," agreed Harrison, much exercised in mind.

"You bet I'm right," Seth assured. "But what I want to talk to you two about is something more important. It's this: what is your real ambition in life?"

Without hesitation, Gleed said, "To ride the spaceways while remaining in one piece."

"Same here," Harrison contributed.

"I guessed that much. You'd not be in the space service if it wasn't your choice. But you can't stay in it forever. All things come to an end. What then?"

Harrison fidgeted uneasily. "I don't care to think of it."

"Some day you'll have to," Seth pointed out. "How much longer have you got?"

"Four and a half Earth-years."

Seth's gaze turned to Gleed.

"Three Earth-years."

"Not long," said Seth. "I didn't expect you'd have much time left. It's a safe bet that any ship penetrating this deeply into space has a crew composed mostly of experienced old-timers getting near to the end of their terms. The practiced hands usually are chosen for the awkward jobs. By the day your boat lands on Terra it will be the end of the trail for many of them, won't it?"

"It will be for me," admitted Gleed, none too happy at the thought of it.

"Time, time, the older you get the faster it goes. Yet when you leave the service you'll still be comparatively young." He put on a faint, taunting smile. "I suppose you'll buy yourself a private space-vessel and continue to roam the cosmos on your own?"

"Don't talk silly," snapped Gleed. "A Moon-boat is the best a very rich man could afford. Puttering to and fro between a satellite and its primary is no fun when you're used to Blieder-zips across the galaxy. The smallest space-going craft is far beyond reach of the wealthiest. Only governments can foot the bill for them."

"By 'governments' you mean communities?"

"In a way."

"Well, then, what are you going to treat yourself to when your space-roaming days are over?"

"I'm not like Big Ears here." Gleed jerked an indicative thumb at Harrison. "I'm a trooper and not a technician. So my choice will be limited by my lack of qualifications." He scratched his head and looked wistful. "I was born and brought up on a farm. I still know a good deal about farming. So I think I'd like to get a small one of my own and settle down."

"Think you'll manage to do it?" asked Seth, watching him intently.

"On Falder or Hygeia or Norton's Pink Heaven or some other planet. But not on Terra. My savings won't extend to that. I couldn't find half enough to meet Earth costs."

"Meaning you can't pile up sufficient obs?"

"I can't," agreed Gleed lugubriously. "Not even if I save until I've got a white beard four feet long."

"So that is Terra's reward for a long, long spell of faithful service—forego your heart's desire or get out?"

"Shut up!"

"I won't," said Seth. "Why do you think four million Gands came here, Doukhobors and Naturists to Hygeia, Quakers and others to all their selected haunts? Because Terra's reward for good citizenship has always been a peremptory order to knuckle down or get out. So we got out."

"It was just as well, anyway," Elissa interjected. "According to our history books Terra was badly overcrowded. We went away and relieved the pressure."

"That is beside the point," reproved Seth. He continued with Gleed. "You want a farm. You can't have it on Terra much as you'd like it there. Terra says, 'No—get out!' So it has to be some place else." He waited for that to sink in, then, "Here, you can have one for the mere taking." He snapped his fingers. "Just like that!"

"You can't kid me," said Gleed with the expression of one yearning to be kidded. "Where are the hidden strings?"

"On this planet any plot of ground belongs wholly to the person in possession, the one who is making actual use of it. Nobody disputes his claim so long as he continues to use it. All you need do is look around for a suitable piece of unused territory—of which there is plenty—and start using it. From that moment it is yours. Immediately you cease to use it and walk out it is anyone else's for the taking."

"No!" said Gleed incredulously.

"Yes!" insisted Seth. "Moreover, if you look around long enough and strike really lucky you might stake first claim to a farm somebody else has abandoned because of death, illness, a desire to move elsewhere, a chance at something he liked better, or any other excellent reason. In that case, you would acquire ground already part-prepared together with farmhouse, milking shed, barns and all the rest. And it would be yours, all yours."

"What would I owe the previous occupant?" Gleed asked.

"Nothing. Not an ob. Why should you? If he isn't buried he has left for the sake of something else equally free. He can't have the benefit both ways, coming and going."

"It doesn't make sense to me. Somewhere there's a snag. Somewhere I've got to pour out hard cash or pile up a lot of obs."

"Of course you have. You start a farm. A handful of local

folk help you to build a house. They dump heavy obs on you. The carpenter wants farm produce for his family for the next two years. You give it, thus getting rid of that ob. You continue giving it for a couple of extra years and thereby plant an ob on *him*. The first time you want fences mended, or some other suitable task done, along he comes to wipe out *that* ob. And so with all the rest including the people who supply your raw materials, your seeds and machinery, or do your trucking for you."

"They won't all want milk and potatoes," Gleed said.

"Don't know what you mean by potatoes. I've never heard of them."

"How can I settle accounts with someone who may be getting all the farm produce he wants from elsewhere?"

"Easily," replied Seth. "A tinsmith fixes you up with several churns. He doesn't want food. He's getting from another source all the stuff he needs. His wife and three daughters are overweight and dieting. The mere thought of a load from your farm gives them the holy horrors."

"Well?"

"But this tinsmith's tailor, or his cobbler, have got obs on him and he's not found the chance to cancel them. So he transfers them to you. As soon as you're able, you give the tailor or cobbler whatever they require to satisfy the obs, thus doing the tinsmith's killing along with your own." Giving his usual half-smile, he added, "And everyone is happy."

Gleed stewed it over, frowning in thought. "You're tempting me. You shouldn't do that. It's a punishable crime to try to divert a spaceman from his allegiance. It's sedition. Terra is tough with sedition."

"Tough my eye!" Seth sniffed contemptuously. "We have Gand laws here."

"All you need do," suggested Elissa, sweetly persuasive, "is say to yourself that you must return to the ship, that it's your bounded duty to do so, that neither the ship nor Terra can get along without you." She tucked a curl away. "Then be a free individual and say, 'I won't.'"

"They'd skin me alive. Bidworthy would preside over the operation in person."

"I don't think so," contradicted Seth. "This Bidworthy—whom I presume to be anything but a jovial character—stands with you and the rest of your crew at the same junction. The road before him splits two ways. He has to take one or the other and there's no third alternative. Sooner or later he'll be hell-bent for home eating his top lips as he goes, or else he'll be trundling around in a truck delivering your milk—because deep down inside himself that's what he's always wanted to do."

"You don't know Ruthless Rufus," mourned Gleed. "He uses a lump of old iron for a soul."

"That's funny," remarked Harrison. "Until today I've always thought of you in the same way."

"I'm off duty," replied Gleed, as if that explained everything. "I can relax and let the ego zoom around outside of business hours." Shoving back his chair, he came to his feet. His eyes were stubborn and his jaw firm. "But I'm going back on duty—right now."

"You're not due before sundown tomorrow," Harrison protested.

"I don't care. I'm going back all the same."

Elissa opened her mouth, closed it as Seth nudged her. They sat in silence as Gleed marched determinedly out.

"It's a good sign," commented Seth, strangely self-assured. "He's been handed a wallop right where he's weakest." Chuckling low down, he turned to Harrison. "What is *your* ultimate ambition?"

Harrison also came to his feet, deeply embarrassed. "Thanks a lot for the meal. It was a good one and I needed it." He made a feeble gesture toward the door. "I'm going to catch him up. If he's returning to the ship I think I'd better do the same."

Again Seth nudged Elissa. They said nothing as Harrison made his way out, carefully closing the door behind him.

"Sheep," decided Elissa, disappointed for no obvious reason. "One follows another. Just like sheep."

"Not so," said Seth. "They are humans animated by the same thoughts and the same emotions as were our forefathers who had nothing sheeplike about them." Twisting around in his chair, he beckoned to Matt. "Bring us two shemaks." Then to Elissa, "We'll drink to sedition. My guess it that it won't pay that ship to hang around too long."

12

The battleship's caller-system bawled imperatively, "Fanshaw, Folsom, Fuller, Garson, Gleed, Gregory, Haines, Harrison, Hope——" and so on down through the alphabet.

A steady trickle of men flowed along the passages, catwalks and alleyways towards the forward chartroom. They gathered outside it in small clusters, chattering in undertones and sending odd scraps of conversation echoing down the corridor.

"Wouldn't say anything to us but, 'Myob!' We became sick and tired of it after a while."

"You should have split up, like we did. That showplace on the outskirts just doesn't know what a Terran looks like. I walked in and took a seat with no trouble at all."

"If ten of you stick together, all in the same uniform, you must expect to be identified on sight. That and your depraved faces is a complete giveaway."

"Did you hear about Meakin? He mended a leaky roof, chose a bottle of double-dith in payment and mopped the lot. He was dead flat when we found him. Snoring like a hog. Had to be carried back."

"Some guys have all the luck. We got the brush-off wherever we showed our faces. Man, it was wearing."

"You should have separated, like I said."

"Half the mess must still be lying in the gutter—they haven't turned up yet."

"Grayder will be hopping mad. He'd have stopped this morning's second quota if he'd known in time."

"When my turn comes the technique will be to get down that gangway and run like hell before they've a chance to call me back."

"Sammy, you'll be mighty lucky if you get a turn."

Every now and again First Mate Morgan stuck his head out of the chartroom doorway and yelled a name already voiced on the caller. Frequently there was no response.

"Harrison!" he bawled.

With a puzzled expression, Harrison went inside. Captain Grayder was there seated behind his desk and gazing moodily at a list lying before him. Colonel Shelton was stiff and erect to one side with Major Hame slightly behind. Both wore the pained look of those tolerating a bad smell while a half-witted plumber searches in vain for the leak.

In front of the desk the Ambassador was tramping steadily to and fro, muttering deep down in his chins. "Barely five days and already the rot has set in." He halted as Harrison entered, fired off sharply, "So it's you, Mister. When did you return from leave?"

"The evening before last, sir."

"Ahead of time, eh? That's curious. Did you get a puncture or something?"

"No, sir. I didn't take my bicycle with me."

"Which is just as well," approved the Ambassador. "If you had done so you'd now be a thousand miles away and still pushing hard."

"Why, sir?"

"Why? He asks me why! That is precisely what I want to know—*why?*" He fumed a bit, then inquired, "Did you visit this town by yourself or in company?"

"I went with Sergeant Gleed, sir."

"Call him," ordered the Ambassador, looking at Morgan. Opening the door, Morgan shouted, "Gleed! Gleed!"

No answer.

He tried again, without result. Once more they put it over the caller-system. The name resounded all over the ship from nose to tail. Sergeant Gleed refused to be among those present.

"Has he signed in?"

Grayder consulted his list. "Yes. In early. Twenty-four hours ahead of time. He may have sneaked out again with the second liberty quota this morning and omitted to put it in the book. That's a double crime."

"If he's not on the ship he's off the ship, crime or no crime."

"Yes, Your Excellency." Grayder registered slight weariness.

"GLEED!" howled Morgan outside the door. A moment later he poked his head within and said, "Your Excellency, one of the men tells me that Sergeant Gleed cannot be aboard because he saw him in town an hour ago."

"Send him in." The Ambassador made an impatient gesture at Harrison. "Stay where you are, Mister, and keep those confounded ears from flapping. I've not finished with you yet."

A tall, gangling grease-monkey came in, blinked around obviously awed by the assembly to top brass.

"What do you know about Sergeant Gleed?" demanded the Ambassador.

The other nervously licked his lips, sorry that he had mentioned the missing man. "It's like this, your honor——"

"Call me 'sir.' "

"Yes, your honor." More disconcerted blinking. "I went out with the second party early this morning but came back a short time ago because my stomach was acting up. On the way here I saw Sergeant Gleed and spoke to him."

"Where?"

"In town, your honor, sir. He was sitting in one of those big, long-distance coaches. I thought it a bit queer."

"Get down to the roots of it, man! What did he tell you, if anything?"

"Not much, sir, your honor. He seemed pretty chipper about something. Mentioned a young widow struggling to look after two hundred acres. Someone had told him about her and he thought he'd take a peek." He hesitated, backed off warily and finished, "He also said that I'd see him in irons or never."

"One of *your* men," said the Ambassador to Shelton. "A hardened space-trooper, allegedly experienced, loyal and well-disciplined. One with long service, three stripes and a pension to lose." His attention returned to the informant. "Did he say exactly where he was going?"

"No, sir, your . . . uh. I asked him but he grinned like an ape and said, 'Myob!' So I came back to the ship."

"All right. You may go." The Ambassador watched the other depart then continued with Harrison. "You were one of that first quota?"

"Yes, sir."

"Let me tell you something, Mister. Over four hundred men went out. About two hundred have returned. Forty of those were in various stages of alcoholic turpitude. Ten of them are locked in the brig yelling, 'I won't' in steady chorus. Doubtless they'll continue to scream it until they've sobered up."

He stared at Harrison as if holding that worthy personally responsible for the mess, then went on, "There is something paradoxical about this situation. I can understand the drunks. There are always a few morons who blow their tops first day on land. But of the two hundred who have condescended to come back about half returned before time, the same as you did. Their reasons were identical: the town was unfriendly, everyone treated them like ghosts until they'd had enough."

Harrison made no comment.

"So we have two diametrically opposed reactions," the Ambassador complained. "One lot of men says the place stinks so much they'd far rather be back on the ship. Another lot finds the town so hospitable that either they get filled to the gills with some horrible muck called double-dith or they stay sober and desert the service. I want an explanation. There has to be one somewhere. You've been twice in this town. What can you tell us?"

Carefully, Harrison said, "It all depends upon whether or

not one is immediately recognizable as a Terran. Also on whether you happen to make contact with Gands who'd rather convert you than give you the brush-off." He pondered a few seconds, added, "Uniforms are a bad factor. The Gands seem to hate the sight of them."

"You mean they're allergic to uniforms?"

"Yes, sir."

"Any idea why?"

"I couldn't say for certain, sir. I don't know enough about them yet. As a guess, I think they may have been taught to associate uniforms with the Terran regime from which their ancestors escaped."

"Escaped? Nonsense!" exclaimed the Ambassador. "They grabbed the benefit of Terran inventions, Terran techniques, and Terran manufacturing ability to go someplace where they'd have more elbow-room." He gave Harrison the sour eye. "Don't any of them wear uniforms?"

"Not that I could recognize as such. They seem to take pleasure in expressing their individual personalities by wearing anything from pigtails to pink boots; oddity in attire is the norm among the Gands. To them, uniformity is the real oddity—they think it's submissive and degrading."

"You refer to them as Gands. From where did they get that name?"

Harrison told him, thinking back to Elissa and her explanation. In his mind's eye he could see her now. And Seth's place with its inviting tables and steam rising behind the counter and mouthwatering smells oozing from the background. Now that he came to visualize the scene again it appeared to embody a subtle, elusive but essential something that the ship had never possessed.

"And this person," he concluded, "invented what they call The Weapon."

"H'm-m-m! And they say he was a Terran, eh? What did he look like? Did you see a photograph or statue?"

"They don't erect statues, sir. They don't consider that any person is more important than any other."

"Bunkum!" snapped the Ambassador, instinctively rejecting that viewpoint. "Did it occur to you to gather any revealing details about him or, at least, find out at what period in history this wonderful weapon first appeared?"

"No, sir," confessed Harrison. "I didn't think it important."

"You wouldn't. Some of you men are too slow to catch a Callistrian sloth wandering in its sleep. I don't critize your abilities as spacemen but as intelligence-agents you're a dead loss."

"I'm sorry, sir," said Harrison.

Sorry? You louse! whispered something deep within his own mind. *Why should you be sorry? He's only a pompous fat man who couldn't cancel an ob if he tried. He's no better than you. Those raw boys prancing around on Hygeia would maintain that he's not as good as you because he's got a pot-belly. Yet you keep staring at his pot-belly and saying, "Sir" and, "I'm sorry." If he tried to ride your bike he'd fall off before he'd gone ten yards. He's just another Terran freak. Go spit in his eye and say, "I won't!" You're not scared, are you?*

"*No!*" announced Harrison, loudly and emphatically.

Captain Grayder glanced up in surprise. "If your're going to start answering questions before they've been asked, you'd better see the medic. Or have we a telepath on board?"

"I was thinking," Harrison said.

"I approve of that," put in the Ambassador. He lugged a couple of huge tomes off the wall-shelves, began to thumb rapidly through them. "Do plenty of thinking whenever you've the chance and it will become a habit. It will get easier and easier in time until eventually a day may come when it can be performed without great pain."

Shoving the books back, he pulled out two more, spoke to Major Hame who happened to be at his elbow. "Don't pose there glassy-eyed like a relic propped up in a military museum. Lend a hand with this mountain of knowledge. I want Gandhi, anywhere from four hundred to a thousand Earth-years ago."

Hame came to life, started dragging out books and searching through them. So did Colonel Shelton. Grayder remained at his desk and continued to mourn the missing.

"Ah, here it is, nearly six hundred years back." The Ambassador ran a plump finger along the printed lines. "Gandhi, sometimes called Bapu, or Father. Citizen of Hindi. Politico-philosopher. Opposed authority by means of an ingenious system called Civil Disobedience. Last remnants disappeared with the Great Explosion but may still persist on some planet out of contact."

"Evidently it does," commented Grayder dryly.

"Civil disobedience," repeated the Ambassador, screwing up his eyes. He had the air of trying to study something turned upside-down and inside-out. "They can't make *that* a social basis. It just won't work."

"It does work," asserted Harrison, forgetting to put in the "sir."

"Are you contradicting me, Mister?"

"I'm stating a fact."

"Your Excellency," put in Grayder, "I suggest——"

"Leave this to me." His color deepening, the Ambassador waved him away. His gaze remained angrily on Harrison. "You are very far from being an expert upon socio-economic problems. Get that into your head, Mister. Anyone of your caliber can be fooled by superficial appearances."

"It works," persisted Harrison, finding cause to marvel at his own stubbornness.

"So does your damnfool bicycle. You've a bicycle mentality."

Something snapped and a voice remarkably like his own said, "Nuts!" Astounded by this phenomenon, Harrison waggled his ears.

"What was that, Mister?"

"Nuts!" he repeated, feeling that what has been done cannot be undone.

Beating the purpling Ambassador to the draw, Grayder stood up, his expression severe, and exercised his own authority.

"Regardless of further leave-quotas, if any, you are confined to the ship. Now get out!"

Harrison departed, his mind in a whirl but his soul strangely satisfied. Outside, First Mate Morgan glowered at him.

"How long d'you think it's going to take me to work through this list of names when guys like you squat in there for a week?" He grunted with ire, cupped hands around his mouth and bellowed, "Hope! Hope!"

No reply.

"Hope's been abandoned," informed Trooper Kinvig.

"That's really funny," sneered Morgan. "Look at me rolling all over the deck." He cupped hands again and tried the next name. "Hyland! Hyland!"

No response.

Four more days, long, tedious, dragging ones. That made nine in all since the battleship formed the rut in which it was still sitting.

There was trouble on board. Put off repeatedly, the third and fourth leave-quotas were becoming impatient, irritable.

"Morgan showed him the third roster again this morning. Same result. Grayder was forced to admit that this world cannot be defined as hostile and that we're legally entitled to run free."

"Well, why the blazes doesn't he keep to the book? The Space Committee could crucify him for ignoring it."

"Same excuse. He says he's not denying leave, he's merely postponing it. That's a crafty evasion, isn't it? He says he'll allow us to go out immediately the missing men come back."

"That might be never. Darn him, he's using them as a pretext to gyp me out of my liberty."

It was a powerful and legitimate complaint. Weeks, months, years of close confinement in a constantly vibrating metal bottle, no matter how big and comfortable, demands ultimate release. Men need fresh air, the good earth, the broad, clear-cut horizon, bulk-food, feminine companionship, new faces.

"He *would* ram home the stopper just when we've learned the best way to get around. Civilian clothes and behave like Gands, that's the secret. Even the first-quota boys are ready for another try."

"Grayder daren't take the risk. He's lost too many men already. One more quota cut in half and he won't have sufficient crew to lift the ship and take it home. We'd be stuck here for keeps. How'd you like that, freak?"

"I wouldn't grieve."

"He could train the bureaucrats to run the ship. It's high time those myopic bums did some honest work."

"That would take three years. Your training lasted three years, didn't it?"

Harrison came along holding a small envelope. Three of them picked on him at sight.

"Look who sauced His Loftiness and got confined to ship—same as us."

"That's what I like about it," observed Harrison. "Better to be fastened down for something than for nothing."

"It won't be for much longer, you'll see! We're not going to hang around bellyaching forever. Mighty soon we'll *do* something."

"Such as what?"

"We're thinking it over," evaded the other, not liking to be taken up so quickly. He noticed the envelope. "What's that you've got there?—the morning mail?"

"Exactly that," Harrison agreed.

"Have it your own way. I wasn't being nosey. I thought perhaps you'd got some more written orders. You engineers usually pick up the paper-stuff first."

"It *is* mail," said Harrison.

"Don't be daft. Nobody receives letters in this part of the cosmos."

"I do."

"Well, how did you get that one?"

"Worrall brought it in from town a few minutes ago. A friend of mine gave him dinner and let him bring the letter to wipe out the ob." He pulled a large ear and smirked at them. "Influence, that's what you boys need."

Showing annoyance, one demanded, "What's Worrall doing off the boat? Is he privileged?"

"In a way. He's married and has three kids."

"So what?"

"The Ambassador figures that some people can be trusted more than others. They're not as likely to disappear, having too much to lose. So a few have been sorted out and sent into town to seek information about the missing ones."

"Have they found out anything?"

"Not much. Worrall says the quest is sheer waste of time. He traced a few of our men here and there, tried to persuade them to return but each said, 'I won't.' The Gands all said, 'Myob!' And that was that."

"There must be something in this Gand business," said one of them thoughtfully. "I'd give a lot to look into it for myself."

"That's what Grayder is afraid of."

"We'll give him more than that to worry about if he doesn't become reasonable pretty soon. Our patience is evaporating fast."

"Mutinous talk," Harrison reproved. He shook his head and displayed great sorrow. "You fellows shock me."

Continuing along the corridor, he reached his tiny cabin, fingered the envelope in pleased anticipation. The writing inside might be feminine. He hoped so. Tearing it open, he had a look. It wasn't.

Signed by Gleed, the missive said, "Never mind where I am or what I'm doing—this note might get into the wrong hands. All I'll tell you is that I expect to be fixed up topnotch providing I wait a decent interval to improve acquaintance. The rest of this directly concerns *you.*"

"Huh?" He lay back on his bunk and held the letter nearer the light.

"I found a little fat guy running an empty shop. He does nothing but sit there waiting. Next, I learned that he has established possession by occupation of the premises. He's doing it on behalf of a factory that makes two-ball rollers, you know, those fan-driven motor-bikes. They want someone to operate the place as a local roller sales and service depot. The little fat man has had four applications to date but none from anyone with engineering ability and experience. The one who eventually gains this post will thereby plant a functional ob on the town, whatever that means. Anyway, this lovely business proposition is measured to your size. It's yours for the taking. Don't be freaky, freak. Jump in with me—the water's fine!"

"Zipping meteors!" said Harrison. His eyes moved on to the footnote at bottom.

"P.S. Seth will give you the address. P.P.S. This place where I am right now is your brunette's home town and she's thinking of coming back. She wants to live near her sister. So do I, man! The said sister is a honey!"

Stirring restlessly, he read it through a second time and a third, got up and paced around the cabin. There were sixteen hundred occupied worlds within the scope of the Terran Empire. He'd seen less than one-twentieth of them. No spaceman could live long enough to visit the lot. The service was divided into cosmic groups each dealing with its own relatively small section of the galaxy.

Except by hearsay—of which there was plenty and most of it highly colored—he would never know what heavens or pseudo-heavens existed in the other sections. In any case, it would be a blind gamble to pick on an unfamiliar world for landbound life solely on somebody else's recommendation. Not all think alike or have the same tastes. One man's meat may be another's poison.

The choice for retirement—which was the ugly name for beginning another, different but vigorous life—was high-priced on Terra or some more desirable planet in his own section. There was the Epsilon group, for instance, fourteen of them, all attractive providing you could suffer the gravity and endure lumbering around like a tired elephant. And there was Norton's Pink Paradise if, for the sake of getting by in peace, you could pander to Septimus Norton's rajah-complex and put up with his delusions of grandeur.

Out near the edge of the Milky Way was a matriarchy bossed by blonde Amazons, and a world of self-styled wizards, and a Pentecostal planet, and a globe where semi-sentient vegetables cultivated themselves in obedience to human masters. All these scattered across many light-years of space but accessible by Bliederdrive.

There were more than fifty known to him by personal experience, though only a tithe of the whole. All offered life and that human company which is the essence of life.

But this world of the Gands had something all the others lacked; it had the quality of being present, in the here and now. It was part of the existing environment from which he drew data on which to build his decisions. The others were not. They lost virtue by being absent and far away.

Quietly he made his way to the Blieder-room lockers, spent an hour cleaning and oiling his bicycle. Twilight was approaching when he returned. Taking a thin plaque from his pocket, he hung it on the wall, lay on his bunk and contemplated it.

F.—I.W.

The caller-system clicked, cleared its throat and announced, "All personnel will stand by for general instruction at eight hours tomorrow."

"I won't," said Harrison, and closed his eyes.

It was seven-twenty in the morning but nobody thought it early. There is little sense of earliness or lateness among space-roamers; to regain it they have to be landbound a month, watching a sun rise and set.

The chartroom was empty but there was considerable activity in the control-cabin. Grayder was there with Shelton and Hame, also chief navigators Adamson, Werth and Yates, and, of course, His Excellency.

There were more than fifty known to him by personal

"I never thought the day would come," groused the latter, scowling at the star map over which the navigators pored. "Less than a couple of weeks and we retreat, admitting complete defeat."

"With all respect, Your Excellency, it doesn't look like that to me," said Grayder. "One can be defeated only by avowed enemies. These people are not enemies. That is where they've got us by the short hairs. They're not definable as hostile."

"That may be. I still say it's defeat. What else can you call it?"

"We've been outwitted by awkward relatives. There's nothing we can do about it. A man doesn't beat up his nephews and nieces merely because they refuse to speak to him."

"That is your viewpoint as a ship's commander. You have been confronted with a situation that requires you to return to base and report. It's routine. The entire space service is hidebound with routine." The Ambassador again eyed the star map as if he considered it offensive. "My own status is different. If I get out without so much as leaving a consul, it's diplomatic defeat, an insult to the dignity and prestige of Terra. I'm far from sure that I ought to go. It might be better if I stayed put even though circumstances would prevent me from functioning effectively and even though my presence would give these Gands endless opportunities for further insults."

"I wouldn't presume to advise you what to do for the best," Grayder said. "All I know is this: we carry troops and armaments for any protective or policing purposes that might be necessary here. But we cannot use them offensively against the Gands because they have provided no real excuse for doing so, also because we cannot influence a government that doesn't exist, and also because our full strength isn't enough to crush a population numbering many millions. We'd need an armada to make an impression upon this world. Even then we'd be fighting at the extreme limit of our reach and the reward of victory would be an area of destruction not worth having."

"Don't remind me. I have examined the problem from every angle until I'm sick of it."

Grayder shrugged. He was a man of action so long as it was action in deep space. Planetary shenanigans were not properly his responsibility. Now that the decisive moment was drawing near, when he would be back in his own attenuated element, he was becoming phlegmatic. To him, the Gand world was a visiting-place among a big number of them. And there were plenty more to come.

"Your Excellency, if you're in serious doubt about remaining here or returning with us, I'd appreciate it if you'd reach a decision fairly soon. First Mate Morgan has given me the tip that if I haven't approved the third leave-quota by ten o'clock the men intend to take matters into their own hands and walk out."

"That kind of conduct would get them into trouble of a really hot kind, wouldn't it?"

"I don't know, really I just don't know," confessed Grayder.

"You mean they can actually defy you and get away with it?"

"Their idea is to turn my own quibbling against me. Since I've said repeatedly that I'm not officially forbidding leave, a walkout cannot be construed as mutiny. As you know, Your Excellency, I have been postponing leave. Therefore the men could plead before the Space Committee that I have ignored regulations. It is quite possible that the plea might succeed if the Space Committee happened to be in the mood to assert its authority."

"The Space Committee ought to be taken on a few long flights," opined the Ambassador. "They'd discover a lot of things they'll never learn behind a desk." He became mockingly hopeful. "How about us accidentally dropping our cargo of bureaucrats overboard on the way home? Such a misfortune should benefit the spaceways if not humanity in general."

"The suggestion strikes me as Gandish," said Grayder.

"The Gands wouldn't think of it. Their one and only technique is to say no, no, a thousand times no. That's all. But to judge by what has happened here it is more than enough." Morosely, the Ambassador pondered his predicament, decided, "I'm coming with you. It goes against the grain because it smacks of abject surrender. To stay would be a defiant gesture but I have to face the fact that it wouldn't serve any useful purpose at the present stage."

"Would you like us to return you to Hygeia?"

"No. The consul there is welcome to that crowd of nakes. Besides, I think I should give Terra the benefit of my personal report about this trip."

"Very well, Your Excellency." Going to a port, Grayder looked through it toward the town. "We have lost approximately four hundred men. Some of them have deserted for keeps. The others will return in their own good time and if I wait long enough. The latter have struck lucky, got their legs under somebody's table and are likely to extend their leave for as long as the fun lasts. They'll come back when it suits them, thinking they may as well be hung for sheep as for lambs. I have that sort of trouble on every long trip. It isn't so bad on the short ones." Moodily he surveyed a terrain bare of returning prodigals. "But we dare not wait for them. Not here."

"No, I reckon not."

"If we hang around much longer we're going to lose another two hundred. There won't be enough skilled men to take the boat up. The only way in which I can beat them to the draw is to give the order to prepare for take-off. They'll all come under flight regulations from that moment." He put on a pained smile. "That will give the space-lawyers among them plenty to think about."

"All right, make the order as soon as you like," approved the Ambassador. He joined the other at the port, studied the distant road, watched three Gand coaches whirl along it without stopping. He frowned, still upset by the type of mind which insists on pretending that a metal mountain is not there. Then his attention turned aside toward the tail-end. "What are those men doing outside?"

Shooting a swift glance in the same direction, Grayder grabbed the caller-microphone and rapped, "All personnel will prepare for take-off at once!" Then he seized his intercom phone and spoke on that. "Who's there? Sergeant Major Bidworthy? Look, Sergeant Major, there are a half a dozen men loafing outside the midway lock. Order them in immediately —we're lifting as soon as everything is ready."

By now the fore and aft gangways had been rolled into their stowage spaces. The midway one swiftly followed. Some fast-thinking quartermaster prevented further escape by operating the midship ladder-wind, thus trapping Bidworthy along with an unknown number of would-be sinners.

Finding himself stalled by the fifty-foot drop, Bidworthy stood in the rim of the airlock and glared at those outside. His mustache not only bristled, but quivered. Five of the objects of his fierce attention had been members of the first leave-quota. One of them was Trooper Casartelli. That got Bidworthy's rag out, a trooper. The sixth was Harrison, complete with bicycle polished and shining.

Searing the lot of them, especially the trooper, Bidworthy grated, "Get back on board. No funny business. We're about to go up."

"Hear that, Mortimer?" asked one, nudging the nearest. "Get back on board. If you can't jump fifty feet you'd better flap your arms and fly."

"No sauce from you," roared Bidworthy. "I have my orders."

"Ye gods, he actually takes orders! At his age!"

Bidworthy scrabbled at the lock's smooth rim in vain search of something to grasp. A ridge, a knob, any kind of projection was needed to help take the strain.

"I warn you men that if you try me too—"

"Quiet, freak."

"Save your breath, Rufus," put in Casartelli. "From now on I'm a Gand." With that, he turned away and walked rapidly toward the road. Four followed him.

Getting astride his bike, Harrison put a foot on the pedal. His back tire promptly sank with a loud *whee-e-e*.

"Come back!" howled Bidworthy at the retreating five. "Come back!" He made extravagant motions, tried to tear the ladder from its automatic grips. A siren keened thinly inside the vessel and that upped his agitation by several ergs.

"Hear that?" His expression murderous, he watched Harrison calmly tighten the rear valve and apply a hand-pump. "We're about to lift. For the last time——"

Again the siren, this time in a rapid series of shrill toots. Bidworthy jumped backward as the airlock seal came down. The lock closed. Harrison again mounted his machine, settled a foot on a pedal but remained watching.

The metal monster shivered from nose to tail then arose slowly and in complete silence. There was stately magnificence in this ascent of such enormous bulk. The ship gradually increased its rate of climb, went faster, faster, became a toy, a dot, and finally disappeared.

For a brief moment Harrison felt a touch of doubt, a hint of regret. It soon passed away. He glanced toward the road.

The five self-elected Gands had thumbed a coach which was now picking them up. That was helpfulness apparently precipitated by the ship's vanishing. Quick on the uptake, these people. He saw it move off on huge rubber balls bearing the five with it. A fan-cycle raced in the opposite direction, hummed into the distance.

"Your brunette," was how Gleed had described her. What had given him that idea? Had she made some remark that he'd construed as complimentary because it had contained no reference to outsize ears?

He had a last look around. The earth bore a great curved rut one mile long by ten feet deep. Two thousand Terrans had been there.

Then about eighteen hundred.

Then sixteen hundred.

Less five.

"One left," he said to himself. "Me."

Giving a fatalistic shrug, he put on the pressure and rode to town.

And then there were none.